7 DEADLY SINS OF REAL ESTATE

Maria Jeanette

I want to celebrate the diverse facets of modern women who are fearlessly redefining social norms within the professional community. These trailblazing women continue to fight passionately for women's right to pleasure, bravely denouncing slut shaming on personal levels, and advocating against the degrading aspects of "cancel culture" amongst black women in professional settings.

Moreover, in the progressive year of 2023, modern women unapologetically engage in sex-positive conversations, empowering and educating others on embracing a healthy and open-minded approach to human sexuality.

Through these pages, we honor the relentless spirit of these women who are breaking barriers, sparking change, and embracing their authentic selves. Let their stories inspire, empower, and remind us all that progress knows no bounds when we stand united for equality and respect in every aspect of life.

Here's to the remarkable modern women shaping a brighter and more inclusive future for us all. May their legacy continue to inspire generations to come. Cheers to the revolution!

Introduction

They say, "You only eat what you kill", but who the fuck is "they" right? Well, it depends on who you ask. In the world of real estate, where you are not only 100% responsible for your own survival, but your own massive success as well. It can be either feast or famine at the hands of YOU. That's a lot of pressure but it can also be exhilarating as fuck! Can you imagine the daily roller coaster of the buyer/seller transaction, agents, brokers, inspectors, lenders, title insurance companies, attorneys, and repair people just to name a few all having to align in order to produce one sale? Shit! I fucking get terrified and aroused at the same damn time just thinking about it. On top of all of that, sometimes you just might have to play the role of friend, counselor, therapist... hell maybe even an accomplice depending on the way the cookie crumbles at a showing. A "quickie" involving a realtor and client in the master bedroom suite and a very irate wife discovering that "sexcapade" comes to mind, but more on that later.

It's no wonder many of us find ourselves slithering right into our carnal desires in excess because adrenaline rushes are a way of life in real estate. We don't play it safe. We take risks all of the damn time and sometimes the amount of money that flows through our fingertips can make even the most limp dick stand rock hard at attention and the driest of pussies release and gush like a New

Orleans levee breaking at the height of Hurricane Katrina. This shit is serious. We play hard and we play for keeps. We can be a peculiar people; lustful, over-indulging, dopamine fiends, power hungry bitches and bastards who can be straight assholes but we can also be the most "happy go-lucky" unrestrained givers you'll ever meet.

We do things to the extreme. We're either all in or out because we need that high. We don't tiptoe around shit, you hear me? We want the full experience because we're going to achieve a win by any means necessary.

I can imagine you're reading this right now like "what kind of book have I picked up?" Listen, I'm just scratching the surface because this is just a preview of what's to come as I take you on a monumental ride of epic proportions. Lust, greed, pride, envy, gluttony, sloth, and wrath; you think you know, but you have absolutely no fucking idea. Where million dollar deals meet BDSM (Bondage and discipline, dominance and submission, sadism and masochism for those who lack the prowess of the sexual underworld), oh we're going there in this erotic tale. All the shit you read in this book is definitely based on some real life experiences. Like I said before, we don't half step at all and this book is no exception. So strap up or strap on, whichever you prefer. These are the seven deadly sins of real estate.

Lust

I've always loved a man in uniform but Frank is actually a real estate developer. He just has the swag of a police officer. You know what I mean; the athletic build, the ability to protect, and that authoritative stance that soaks my panties every single time. Frank is a Pisces so he's typically very direct, a bit snappy, but he's such a hard worker. Whenever Frank comes to mind, I find myself in a bit of a trance. Just the thought of his big black curved dick and how he has the ability to hit my g-spot every single time literally leaves me speechless. Here's the caveat though. He's married, and he ain't married to some pitiful, homely looking bitch either. The chick is bad, you hear me? She's all about appearances though, but she's a doting wife as well. She's a five star mom who literally attends all of her children's functions, games, and whatever else they may be involved in at any given moment. She's also a certified boss in her own right as a premier party planner.

Honestly, I thought they were a picturesque family. Their love was practically cemented at an HBCU many years ago as they were college sweethearts. They might as well have a plaque of themselves in one of those illustrious halls due to how much his wife represents their alma mater every chance she gets. Like I said, they seem to check all of the boxes; smart, educated, beautiful, family oriented, and paid. They really appeared to be the picture of perfection, that is, until Frank slid in my DM one day.

"I think you're beautiful."

That was literally the direct message I'd received from Frank via Facebook back in 2021. Clearly, we were still in the wake of a global pandemic so the thirst was real. To feel the warmth of a woman's body and of course a wet pussy, I'd assumed was his goal. At least that's what I thought until I perused Mr. Frank's profile and noticed he had a whole ass wife and kids. I mean they seemed pretty happy but then again, I'd been married twice so I knew the deal.

Social media ain't shit when it comes to all of these so-called jovial couples. You don't even have to dig deep anymore to figure out it's all a facade because they're creeping their way into the inboxes of many across the world with no shame. I swear, matching pajamas is a dead giveaway for the desolate and lifeless marriages. I can't believe they actually want you to buy into that shit.

Anyway, I entertained Frank because, why not? He was sexy, husky, but not fat, and he oozed big dick energy, which is what drew me in but also our banter was quite intriguing. For two whole weeks, we talked for hours on end about any and everything before we had our first date. I was curious about what he had to offer and I wanted to know more. During the time we were communicating, I had to go out of town on business but as soon as I returned, we scheduled some time for our first in person encounter. We met for breakfast at a quaint spot right outside of the city. As soon as I parked my car, I sensually walked over to him while accentuating my curves with every step. He greeted me at the door of the restaurant with a smile and without hesitation, I grabbed his neck and put my tongue down his throat.

"Damn, you don't waste no time do you?" Frank said while appearing to be caught off guard, but also excited as well.

"Ain't no time to waste." I said seductively.

It really didn't take long before I found myself bent over plenty hotel beds and letting him pound my fucking brains out after that. I just figured he wanted something different. His wife was very poised and polished, but a bitch like me? Well, I knew the struggle all too well even though I didn't look like it. I could move in absolutely any circle you positioned me in. I knew street life as well as corporate life which is probably what made me such a fiery lover for Frank. I could tell he was mesmerized by me and literally could not get enough of me.

Frank and I quickly began doing business together. He was a first generation millionaire real estate developer who owned a widely successful trucking company. He was extremely anal and meticulous with regards to his business dealings, and quite honestly, he was a flat out jerk at times. He was just extremely hard to please but that helped me step my game up even more as an up and coming broker in the Midwest.

There was this one time I was assisting Frank with purchasing some real estate as we had a full day ahead viewing properties. I wasn't exactly the most punctual person as I'd pulled up to the first location a little late, and as usual, Frank was early. I quickly got out of my car, and lightly ran over to Frank as I didn't want to trip and fall in my new Louboutin heels.

"Good morning Frank." I said while a bit winded.

"Hopefully, you're not wasting my time with this shit." Frank states dryly.

"Listen Frank, I really need you to trust the buying process. Real estate is a marathon, not a sprint okay?" I tried my best to educate him but not belittle him.

Frank gets out of his car, slams the door, slowly walks over to me, looks me dead in my eyes and begins speaking to me in a rather elevated tone.

"I need everything to be a fucking sprint you hear me? I have absolutely nowhere to put my trucks and I'm paying double to park at a temporary lot. This shit is for the birds!"

My heart started pounding just a bit because I really needed to close this deal. Yes, I liked him but I also needed this win. My own mortgage payment depended on it. To say that I was terrified was an understatement. We approached the building and Frank opened the door for me because well, he's still a gentleman amidst his apparent frustration.

"I don't fucking like this and it looks like a piece of shit. You can't be fucking serious. Hell, my smallest trucks can't even fit in here. Dammit! Only a goofy would pick something like this MJ. If you want to continue to do business with me, you must do better because I really don't have a problem firing your ass." Frank said after we'd literally just stepped foot inside the property.

"Damn Frank! I'm doing the best I can but I assure you, I won't rest until you get exactly what you're looking for. Look, we have two more properties to see and I truly have a gut feeling that one of these locations will be the one." I tried to convince him.

We left the first property and I swiftly ran to my car praying at the same time that my assistant got the next one right. Lord knows how much I needed this deal. Frank followed me closely in his car to our next stop. When we arrived at the next location, Frank and I parked our cars and approached an in-house listing that I previously had on my schedule for us to view. This time, Frank at least walked around the building and asked specific questions. I observed him examining, scanning, and scrutinizing every bit of the property.

"I actually like this MJ. How much we talking?" Frank was direct and went straight for the obvious question which was the cost.

"So this one is ten million which I know is five million over your proposed budget, but I truly believe with the extra space of this location, you can most certainly make the money back." I tried persuading him.

"Hmmm... I do see your vision but let's take a look at the other property before I make my decision."

"Okay great."

I was hopeful after Frank's response. I knew that I had not yet received the green light from him but it felt like we were at least getting warmer. I would've loved to have sealed this deal of course, but patience was definitely a virtue considering I was still pretty new to this caliber of clientele in real estate.

We got in our cars for what I was hoping would be the last time and made our way over to the last and final property for the day. As I gripped my steering wheel tight and drove a bit over the speed limit, I began praying out loud that Frank would like this listing and that I would be able to get him under contract sooner rather than later. I was depleted at this point. I had been in search of the perfect property for him for quite some time now.

We'd arrived at the last location on my list and before heading in, I checked the mirror to touch up my makeup while attempting to brush the proverbial frustration off of my face. I said out loud to myself, *Maria, you got this shit. Sell it and write that damn contract today!* I was so serious about closing this deal. I was in the fourth quarter at this point and I refused to go into overtime. I took a deep breath and got out of my car. Frank and I locked eyes and something about the way he looked at me indicated we were really in this together. Throughout this whole process, I'd always felt like I was trying to impress him and not just from a business standpoint but a personal one as well. I really needed to close this deal but I also really liked him. To my surprise, as soon as we walked in the building together, immediately he was sold.

"Now this is what I'm talking about." Frank said while appearing to perk up even more than the last showing.

I closely watched his eyes inspect and study the entire place so intently.

"I like this MJ. Let's propose an offer of thirty million." Frank said calmly and matter of factly. Everything seemed to happen so quickly.

I couldn't believe it! I was so shocked that I asked him to repeat himself. This would be the biggest deal of my career and I would be able to pay off my debt. But reality quickly set in as I had been taught not to ever count the deal until it's closed. I gathered myself and calmly stated that I was on it and that I would have his contract drawn up before the end of the day.

Once I got back into my car, I let out a sigh of relief that was followed by a loud exhale of excitement. I put the music on blast and started singing to it. I didn't care who was watching as they walked past because I was about to get paid!

* * *

Today was closing day and it still felt like a dream. Frank and I were expected to meet with the attorney to sign the documents and hopefully, open up a nice bottle of Dom Pérignon champagne to commemorate this lengthy, yet rewarding experience.

The closing was scheduled to take place at Erin's home office. Erin was my go-to real estate attorney for all of my clients, but specifically for my commercial real estate properties. The cool thing about Erin was she was one of my closest friends as well. She knew me inside and out and she definitely knew about the never ending rendezvous I'd been having with Frank. She also helped me clean up a mess or two when Frank's wife, Arianna started suspecting he was cheating. Erin was basically my personal Olivia Pope that I had stored in my back pocket so doing the closing at her home instead of her professional office was unconventional but very necessary.

"Hey boo." I greeted Erin with the longest hug when she opened the door to her luxurious penthouse.

Erin knew how much this deal meant to me. She was well aware of the history between Frank and I which is why this day felt extremely gratifying.

"Honey, you coming up in here looking like a million bucks! Clearly, someone is ready to close the biggest deal of her career to date!" Erin said with much pride and support that's only offered from someone who has had your back since day one. Erin grabbed my hand and ushered me into her home like a big sister guiding a younger sibling to protection. She always looked out for me in so many ways.

Erin's home was palatial as she resided in Streeterville, which is a neighborhood located in the Near North Side of Chicago, also home to the historic Navy Pier and the Museum of Contemporary Art. She had an unparalleled view of Lake Michigan. She walked around her home in designer African caftans when she wasn't working because she was so proud of her Nigerian roots even though she'd assimilated to Western society quite effortlessly.

Erin's taste was almost sinful as her home was adorned with the finest African art that indicated its distinction. And the backsplash of color on the walls made the place pop like 3D dexterity. Everything in her home was top-tier from her dishes to her djembe drum that belonged to her deceased father which appeared to be more like accent furniture than a family heirloom. Let's just say it was a whole lot of money in this motherfucker. Erin was definitely in a class by herself.

I sat on Erin's designer sofa while awaiting Frank's arrival. Erin handed me a glass of red wine and smiled.

"I can't believe this is really happening, Erin." I squealed with excitement after taking a sip of my wine.

"Well, believe it honey. You've earned this." Erin said while slipping in and out of her Nigerian accent and toasting our glasses.

"All I know is that the ink can't dry fast enough once those papers are signed. I've got some bills to pay, no lie. I wonder when Frank will get here. He's typically not late." I said nervously.

As soon as I looked at the time on my phone, the buzzer to Erin's home sounded.

"That must be him." Erin quickly grabbed the door.

When Frank walked in, butterflies filled my stomach. He looked so fucking sexy with his freshly shaved beard, clean bald head, and slightly visible print when I looked at him down below. He was wearing what looked to be a custom fitted suit to indicate he was ready to seal the deal so to speak. I stood up and when he hugged me, I caught a whiff of his cologne that always captivated me. His bear hug made me sink in his arms in addition to causing a bit of a flood between my thighs. He greeted me with a kiss on my cheek.

"Hmmm, I can tell you aren't wearing any panties." Frank whispered in my ear.

I guess when I got up from the sofa, the excitement mixed with the natural movement of my black Gucci skirt shifted in a way to which he caught a quick peek. But I didn't care at all because I was weak for this man and he still made me blush like a schoolgirl.

"Well, seeing that we're all here, we can get this party started." Erin said while positioning the documents in sequential order with a pen in hand.

"Hey hun, I'm going to head to your bathroom while you all are working on that." I said to Erin while trying to be a bit more conscious of my skirt rising this time once I'd gotten up from the sofa.

"Sure babe, take your time. We'll be here." Erin said while focusing on thoroughly reviewing the documents with Frank.

I continued to admire Erin's home while appreciating her consistent hospitality. I spent a bit more time in her bathroom as I'd always loved a beautiful bidet. Her bathroom was enormous. It was practically the size of a master bedroom suite. It came in quite handy as well seeing that I was extremely wet by just the thought of Frank having his way with me. I washed my hands, checked my lipstick, and proceeded to head back to the living room but as soon as I opened the door, Frank was standing right in front of me.

"Whew, you scared me." I said as I was a bit caught off guard.

"I want you back in this bathroom." Frank said intensely.

He grabbed my waist and forcely pushed it towards his and began tonguing me down. He then picked me up and started carrying me back into the bathroom, closing the door with his foot. He propped me up in between the double sinks and thrusted his dick inside my wet pussy but immediately took it right out.

"Wait, why did you stop?" I was definitely begging for it at this point.

"Naw babe, I saw that clean, bald pussy when I snuck a peek earlier. I need to taste all that shit first."

Frank feasted like the last supper and gave me multiple orgasms that made my eyes roll to the back of my head and the hairs on my neck stand up. Once he knew I was satisfied by his immaculate oral capabilities, he put his dick inside me and began working his magic stick like the houdini he was. I thought we had great sex before, but closing sex was a different beast for sure. I began to clench and I could feel myself getting ready to explode. Frank's dick became harder and before I knew it, we were literally having an orgasm at the same time.

"Hey you guys! Funding is here." Erin yelled from the other room as we could hear her footsteps coming up the stairs in the middle of us climaxing.

We were quickly brought back to reality from the fantasy we'd just lost ourselves in.

Whew, that man is fucking amazing, I said to myself.

* * *

Oh my God, I can't believe I'm still in this bed staring at the clock. I've got so much shit to do including what seems like a massive list of showings today. Since the pandemic, all I've been getting are sellers and I need buyers.

It had also been three days since Frank's closing in addition to that porn episode we had in Erin's house and I have not heard from him since. Like what the fuck? He hadn't returned any of my calls or texts. I mean, I know he gotta deal with Suzie Homemaker over there but shit, I had needs too. I know he better not be ghosting me after the way I fucked his brains out.

Oh well, my new favorite toy was just delivered yesterday so I might as well see what that do. While opening the pretty purple and gold box, with a huge kool-aid smile plastered on my face, it felt like Santa was visiting me quite early this year.

I decided to have my new waterproof vibrator accompany me in the shower and whew, that toy provides an experience. When I stepped out of the shower and dried myself off, I noticed my phone was ringing. I quickly grabbed it off of the sink and it slipped out of my wet hands.

"Dammit!" I said aloud as I was hoping I didn't crack the screen on my phone.

Thankfully, I didn't but I almost missed whoever the unknown call was from.

"Hello. This is MJ speaking." I said with a professional tone.

"I'm about to send you a text with an address once we get off of the phone. Meet me there at 7:30 pm wearing black, preferably a dress." Frank said and then quickly hung up before I could say anything.

Frank was so fucking rude. He hadn't called me in three days and then proceeded to just tell me what to do. He got on my damn nerves but he also made me wet at the sound of his voice. Welp, I knew I was about to speed through my day so I could see what Mr. Frank had in store.

Before I knew it, time had flown and I could tell I would be running late because I didn't get back home until seven that evening. I hurried and changed my clothes into a sexy black number that I felt Frank would highly appreciate while making his dick hard at the same time. I swiftly finished my makeup, hopped in my Range Rover, and sped down 157 to whatever this unique location Frank wanted me to grace my presence at. I turned the music up, clicked the button to open my panoramic sunroof, and jammed out to a Jill Scott tune.

I was definitely feeling myself as my mind began to wander with thoughts of what it would be like to actually be Frank's woman. Who was I kidding? He'd been married for ions, had five kids, and I doubt he was going to give all that up for me. He told me Arianna was well aware of the many sexual encounters he'd had with other women while they had been married. I took that as she was pretty loyal and was very satisfied with how Frank significantly funded the lifestyle she'd grown so accustomed to. I'd assumed she didn't want to make waves.

The address was located in an industrial district and for a minute, I wondered if my GPS had sent me off. I got out of my car and quickly walked to the door because I couldn't quite make out where I was. I didn't want to draw too much attention to myself, especially with the way I was dressed. After I pushed the buzzer, a big cock diesel looking motherfucker answered the hard steel door.

"Yes, Frank is awaiting you." The security guard said with a serious tone.

I slowly walked in trying to scope out the scene. I was so confused walking down the hallway until I heard Tank's song, "When We" playing a little low and then the volume increased as I got closer to the entryway. Oh shit, this was a sex party. I definitely wasn't expecting this tonight but it made perfect sense as to why he wanted me to wear this dress along with the cryptic phone call and secret location he sent via text.

I walked into the dimly lit room and I saw people mingling but also slobbing each other down. To my right was a man in a black g-string with a ball gag in his mouth getting slapped on the ass by a busty dominatrix and to my right was a very voluptuous woman handling two dicks like a champ, one in her mouth and one in her ass. I continued to walk around the room and then I saw Frank from afar. As soon as someone moved out of my front view, I saw what appeared to be Arianna standing next to him. He'd shown me a picture of her before because he wanted me to be aware of what she looked like if I ever needed to dodge her. But why the hell was she here?

I tried to compose myself because I honestly didn't know if she knew about me and I didn't want to give anything away. I noticed her walking closer to me until she was standing right in front of me. I didn't know whether to square up or just take the L, but then she smiled at me and reached for a hug.

"I know you fucked my husband. We're a team and so it's my turn now." Arianna whispered in my ear.

What the fuck had I'd gotten myself into? I thought to myself.

Greed

The evening was absolutely gorgeous, until Frank and Arianna decided to interfere on a very special night I had planned for my new boo James. Don't get me wrong, I had some very salacious times with the two of them, but the amount of drama they brought to my life was too much. I had no clue it would go down like that when our relationship first began to unfold.

When I realized Arianna's intentions that night at the sex party, I knew I was in for a wild ride. Our first three-way encounter included Frank and I dancing slowly while he strategically raised my dress at the same time, tickling my clit causing me to engorge. I was already moist upon the sight of him, but his fingers perusing my pussy lips caused me to start dripping like a leaky faucet. I closed my eyes as I allowed him to continue to dance with me while his fingers did all of the talking. Then I felt a hand grace my calves. I looked down, and it was Arianna kissing my legs and moving upward. Before I knew it, she began eating my pussy under my dress while Frank had his tongue down by throat and was grabbing my ass. Goddamn, this was an experience! Just when I thought I'd done it all, they were both pleasuring me like the fucking goddess I knew I was. Needless to say, the amount of juices that bonded us that night was unreal.

And of course, there were many other sexual encounters between the three of us that always left me speechless. I enjoyed every bit of it, but what I enjoyed more was the ongoing business Frank and I did together because the money that started to fill my bank account was sometimes more titillating than the multiple orgasms. Hell, I liked money and I made no apologies for that but when I noticed how obsessed Frank and Arianna started to become with me, that's when I knew I needed to somehow dissolve whatever we had going on. It had gotten to the point where they were showing up to my home unannounced talking about they were just in the neighborhood. And my dumbass gave Frank a spare key to my home one time but I asked him to never just use it unless I wanted to role play. I know, some stupid shit I decided while intoxicated but he'd always respected my space until tonight.

I told Frank and Arianna a couple of months ago that I was no longer interested in having a relationship with the both of them. Between their own family drama that arose, Arianna's mental health issues that started to come to the surface, and Frank's fucking attitude, I said enough is enough. The both of them began blowing up my phone when I told them it was over but Arianna was the worse out of the two of them. It's like she became hypnotized by my pussy or something. She would send me texts asking me if she could eat me out on my period because she wanted to be that much closer to me. Yeah, I was thinking I don't know what kind of fetish this is but I cannot. Frank's aggression also became more obvious when he started sending me texts about his fantasies that involved more abuse than erotica. I changed my number on their asses and didn't look back, but I never thought they would actually use the fucking spare key.

James and I had been together for a little bit but we connected on a deeper level instantly. He was a very handsome lender who I'd actually met not too long before I met Frank. I decided to sort of leave James in the wind but he was convinced that I would be his woman one day.

Well, basically that day was here so in a sense we picked up where we left off.

James was such a go-getter and he knew he was a winner which is why he was pretty convinced I would be in his life. He was arrogant as hell, but he was also very charming. Clearly, I had a type. He definitely had a way with words and women flocked to him with ease. He was the pretentious type as he exuded excellence in everything that he did. He loved playing golf, smoking cigars, he had a shit load of money, and he absolutely loved women. But he treated them more like property and he also used them to get money. I could tell he really liked me but he had absolutely no qualms about telling me that he wanted to pimp me out to get business from the highest bidders and because I was so greedy, I happily obliged.

It was James' birthday, and as lavish as he could be, he told me he wasn't quite in the mood for an extravagant celebration this year. We'd also been out all day networking and making some major power moves together businesswise. Instead, I decided to hire a personal chef to prepare a meal for us as well as a massage therapist to help him relax. I also paid for a happy ending which would be a surprise to him. I was never intimidated by other women in that way and honestly, the way James' stamina was set up, trust me he could enjoy a happy ending and pleasure me right after as well; which is actually what he did.

When the massage therapist arrived at my home, she was just his type. She was a dark-skinned beauty with big breasts and a big ass. Her skin was that of milk-chocolate and she had the most beautiful smile. While James was receiving his massage, I politely walked in just to get a peek as I was a bit turned on by watching her rub James' body. He was lying on his stomach at the time and the massage therapist began working her way down to his hips. I could tell James was becoming a bit tense because he wasn't sure how far the massage therapist would go and he didn't know how comfortable I would be with that. Little did he know, I hired this woman for that very reason. I gave James a look to indicate that it was okay for him to enjoy himself and that's when I noticed his body relax even more and the massage therapist began playing with his ass and then she began to lick it. I walked over to him and whispered in his ear, "Babe, it's okay. Happy birthday and I love you." And then I politely moved out of the way so that the massage therapist could continue her work while I took my voyeuristic stance. I was getting more and more turned on as the motions from James' body indicated he was enjoying himself.

With a sensual voice, she asked James to turn over on his back and that's when she poured some massage oil onto his dick which led to a pretty assertive hand job, and then she began to suck his dick and to my surprise, with no gag reflexes. She literally had his dick and balls in her mouth at the same time and then began to slip her tongue up and down his perineum. And when a man allows himself to let go and enjoy the sensation of getting licked right in between his balls and his anus? Shiiiittt, he'll go crazy even though he'll probably never admit it, nor ask for it. I knew I would definitely be adding that move to my sexual repertoire with James. The intense look on his face while she pleasured him was very exciting to witness and then he looked over at me and mouthed, "thank you" while I was touching myself to a rhythm that was in sync with the movement of her mouth sliding up and down his dick.

By this time, the massage therapist had taken her shirt off, her titties completely exposed, and her pants were a little under her waist revealing the top of her thong. James was massaging her ass more aggressively as she continued to deep throat him. His hips continued to sway and this nigga's toes started to curl as I could tell he was getting ready to blow. When the massage therapist could tell he was about to cum, she opened her mouth wide to receive all of him. James couldn't contain himself and jizzed on her face, in her mouth, and her chest and she took all that shit in like a champ too. I almost busted one myself from just watching them and I enjoyed every minute of it!

I figured after the massage therapist provided James with that happy ending and she began getting dressed, I would take it upon myself to finish myself off but James wasn't having it. He tipped the massage therapist handsomely, sent her on her way, picked me up and carried me onto my bed and began fucking my brains out. I was pleasantly surprised he had it in him after what he'd just received. I really pitied anyone who was not getting fucked like this because it was simply fantastic.

We continued to fuck like jack rabbits until I thought I heard some footsteps. Clearly I was buzzed and was just imagining things. My eyes were closed but I could've sworn I felt someone looking over me and when I opened my eyes, I screamed so loud but not from an intense orgasm. It was Frank and Arianna standing in our room!

"What the fuck are you doing?" Frank said with a stern voice while standing next to Arianna.

This quickly started feeling like it was developing into some fatal attraction shit.

"So yeah, ya'll need to get the fuck out of my house before I call the police." As I started reaching for my piece on the side of my bed.

* * *

I'll never forget the night I met MJ. I'd recently launched my new mortgage company and my goal was to garner the attention of more female realtors to increase my sales and business relationships. I had absolutely no shame in my game. I worked hard all the time and I was determined to get a sale by any means necessary even if I had to leverage the power of the pussy to get it.

One of my good female friends had invited me to a singles mixer for realtors that night. I wasn't really interested in going at the time but I figured I'd attend in order to attract the caliber of realtors I wanted for my company. I walked over to the bar, flirted with the sexy bartender whose titties were definitely representing on the "Double D" side of the game and ordered a scotch neat. The bartender was flirting while hitting me with the 360 so I could see what she was working with from behind. I couldn't help but laugh to myself a little bit. Life was good, I couldn't even front.

When she placed my drink down in front of me, I started thinking about the many female realtors I'd fucked in the ass over the years. No lie, that shit was amazing when we would close a deal together. That was kind of my thing when it came to asserting my dominance but I wasn't a pillow talker and I definitely didn't need to boast about my sexual conquests. During the day, I was all about my business, some might even call me a bit bourgeoisie due to my style and taste. Yes, I wore tailored suits, dined at the finest of restaurants, and kept a very sexy housekeeper on deck, but when it was time to fuck, I liked that nasty shit. A woman that could be classy as ever but an oral beast in the bedroom was definitely my speed. I didn't have time for that prissy shit when it was time to get down and dirty. I hadn't met a woman like that in a while. They were either sexy as hell but too conservative in the bedroom or a downright freak but ghetto as shit in everyday life. I was looking to meet my match.

My thoughts were interrupted when I looked over and saw MJ walking towards the bar. Honestly, I was smitten. She stood about five foot nine inches with incredible legs, her skin was a smooth dark chocolate, she was curvaceous as hell, and she walked with confidence and a hint of pompousness. I knew right then, I needed her on my team in more ways than one. She gave me a look like she'd recognized me but I had never seen her before.

MJ sat down next to me and gave me a half smile like she wanted to talk but was a bit frustrated about something.

"Hello. You look very beautiful this evening. My name is James." I said while slightly moving in a little closer to her.

"Thank you. I'm MJ. I'm sorry, today just ain't my day. My client fired me for someone else, my deal just completely blew up, and I'm just not feeling it tonight. I'm usually not like this. I really just need a fucking drink tonight." MJ said while looking defeated.

"I'm sorry to hear that. Listen, I'll take care of that for you. What would you like?" I asked while trying to figure out more about this mystery woman.

"I'll take a scotch neat." MJ said with a bit of assertiveness.

All I could think to myself was this chick was already certified in my eyes by the drink she ordered. Yeah, I knew I was going to hit that. There was no way on God's green earth I wasn't.

"Excuse me baby, another scotch neat but for the lady this time." I said to the bartender even though I could sense a bit of enviousness in her eyes.

"Oh wow, you making these bitches go crazy like that?" MJ chuckled.

"Oh, I see you got a bit of a pouty mouth. It's kind of sexy. I like it." I was even more intrigued.

"Well, that's me. No holds barred." Maria took a sip of her drink and smiled at me as if she knew what kind of time I was on.

We continued to talk for hours. We definitely didn't do any mixing and mingling with anyone else that night. We just continued to enjoy each other's company. We would kind of lock eyes from time to time and I would find myself gazing at her body up and down. Yep, my dick was getting hard by just the energy of this woman. When I finally looked at my watch, it was already midnight and the bar was closing but I really didn't want her to leave.

"I saw you look down at your watch James. What time is it?" MJ said with a curious tone.

"It's midnight."

"Oh shit, yeah I gotta go. I was enjoying myself so much that I didn't even pay attention to the time. I have an early showing tomorrow morning. I've got to get out of here." MJ grabbed her purse, got up from her seat, and gave me a quick peck on the cheek. Damn, she smelled so good.

"Wait, when can I see you again?" I lightly grabbed MJ's arm feeling like a bit of a simp but I was digging this woman.

"I'll be honest James. With my schedule, I'm not sure. Here's my card. Send me an email and we'll set something up. I really have to go." Before I could say anything, she was practically out the door.

I could tell she wanted me. Her body language the entire evening said it all but clearly she wasn't trying to get into anything right now. Women can be so confusing sometimes. Pussy practically be roaring but they want to play hard to get or they're trying to figure out how to get over the last nigga that did them wrong. But I was convinced I would see her again. I was even more convinced I would get some of that. It was just a matter of time.

* * *

Today I was prepping for a high end networking event I was hosting that I wanted MJ to participate in. We had pretty much become inseparable at this point but it did not happen initially. After we'd met about a year ago at the singles mixer, we were really feeling each other but she had some other guy in the wings she had been dealing with. I already knew what that was about. I mean MJ was a bad motherfucker and I could tell she had options like myself but

I wasn't tripping off that at all. As a matter of fact, I actually told her I would wait for her because I knew she would be back.

Now when I said I would wait for her, I wasn't talking about not fucking other bitches. I mean, come on. But she was different. She was sexy as fuck but she was also solid, smart, quick on her feet, and she had a little bit of gangsta in her. She was also a very beautiful woman inside and out. I saw a really bright future ahead of her as an up and coming broker in the game so even if we didn't hook up initially, I knew she was definitely someone I would want to work with. We didn't really keep in contact much after that singles mixer until about a few months ago when we bumped into each other at another networking event. We pretty much picked up where we left off. Conversations became more consistent, we noticed we had so much in common, and not too long after, MJ was riding me until my eyes rolled to the back of my head. I knew she was the shit but I didn't know she would've surpassed the many other women on my roster. She quickly became one of my top three for sure.

I started really coaching her and molding her into a very keen businesswoman. I began to put her up on game and she quickly became my muse. I was definitely ready to introduce her to the big leagues at this event tonight. She was more than ready and I was pretty certain it wouldn't take much to convince her.

I trained her well because she had all the right ingredients to assist me at this event. Her appearance alone commanded attention, she had the real estate lingo down to a science, and she studied the vernacular of the clientele that I typically attracted. In a sense, she was a triple threat.

I was a big proponent of doing more showing than telling so I made sure that tonight's event would take place at a luxurious mini mansion that set the stage for the kind of clientele my business was aligned with. When it comes to selling luxury real estate, it's all about telling the story. The buyer has to connect with the property and that's where I come in with ensuring that I do extensive research on my target market and that I formulate a compelling argument as to why a home should be their next purchase. But it has to feel like a no-brainer for the buyer almost as if they would be an absolute fool to pass it up because it spoke to them on all levels.

I like when this is strongly demonstrated visually which is why I was hosting this networking event at one of the many properties I raved about.

The upscale property was nestled into a natural oasis in Oak Brook which was a southwest suburb of Chicago, with very easy access into the city. It boasted of premium materials such as granite countertops, marble floors, leaded glass casement windows, state of the art appliances, and smart technology throughout the entire home so that it made living there as easy as possible. The exterior elegance of the home included impeccable landscaping, a large deck that was perfect for any sized gathering, as well as amazing water features such as a beautiful pond that extended quite far into the backyard.

As the house began to fill with attendees, a trio I'd hired was playing some classical jazz music in the background, the hors d'oeuvres were prepared by one of my favorite chefs, and the ambiance throughout the seven bedroom, six bathroom home just tied everything together.

I was having a brief conversation with one of my business partners when MJ arrived. As soon as she stepped foot into the house, it was as if time stopped and all eyes were on her. She'd recently hired a stylist that took her entire look to the next level and I could see the confidence she exuded because of it. I also made sure that whenever she would represent me, every strand of hair was in place, her makeup was flawless, and her manicures and pedicures were pristine. This was my brand and I didn't fuck around when it came to the work I put into it. I wanted all the money because I was greedy as hell but in order to secure the kind of clients I had, everything had to say that I not only had the best properties, but I had the best women to accompany them as well. And I was getting ready to introduce MJ to the other side of the real estate game tonight.

"Hey babe, I made it! I know I'm a tad bit late, but honey, I always am." MJ said a little winded while giving me a hug.

"So here's the deal, that tardiness shit stops today. We talked about this. And while we're out in public, let's kind of slow down on the public displays of affection. I need you to be the boss that you are so act like it." I whispered sternly in her ear.

I knew that she would think I was hard on her but she knew my standards with regards to business and I needed her to be extremely on point today.

"Babe, damn, you can be so harsh." MJ said while looking a bit hurt.

"Look, babe, I get it. You know I got you but right now, we gotta come correct. We talked about this. But come with me, there's a few people I want to introduce you to."

I placed my hand at the small of MJ's back and guided her over to some business associates of mine.

We made small talk throughout the evening and I could tell MJ was in her element with how she worked the room. I was definitely proud to see her step into the fierce businesswoman I knew she was destined to be. I watched all the men eye her up and down just wishing to get a taste of what I'd experienced with her behind closed doors. It came with a price though and I was definitely willing to sell MJ to the highest bidder.

"Babe, this place is lit with money." MJ whispered to me with excitement.

"Oh trust me, it gets a lot sweeter. So here's what's going to happen this evening. It was definitely by design some of the men I introduced you to. I have some big things coming up that I want your assistance with. These deals could change your life and make us so much fucking money but I need to know that you're really down." I said with conviction.

"Yes, babe. I told you I was. Whatever it is, I'll do it." MJ said with such trust in her eyes.

"When the event ends tonight around ten-thirty, I want you to go upstairs to the master bedroom. We'll call it room seven for kicks. The door will actually be locked but there's a bell that's installed for that room only. I want you to ring it and wait for someone to answer." I said cryptically.

"Uum, James what the hell are you talking about?" MJ appeared concerned.

"You trust me don't you?"

"Of course I do. But I'm just trying to figure out what's going on."

"Listen, you told me you would be my partner in this and we are literally about to make so much money but in order for us to do that, I need you to demonstrate more than just your real estate skills. We talked about this so what I need you to do is——"

Before I could finish my sentence, MJ grabbed my hand and whispered in my ear, "I got you boss" and then she kissed me on my neck discreetly. My dick was so hard when she said that to me. I knew she was ready for this but damn! I had to tuck my shit in to keep everyone from seeing the effect she had on me. But who was I kidding, how was I really gonna hide this big dick?

When MJ walked off, she looked back at me as if she knew I was watching her fat ass walk away. I watched her continue to work the room, but I had to get back focused because she was turning me the fuck on. I continued to network while I signaled to my secretary to review the non-disclosure agreements I had the potential suitors sign upon their arrival.

As time went on, guests started to leave one by one for the evening and I overheard their conversations stating how much they enjoyed the event until the very last person left. The only two people who remained were myself and MJ.

"So babe, you ready?" I asked MJ in a supportive tone.

"Ready as I'll ever be." MJ said nervously.

"Look, you've got this. I wouldn't position you for this if you weren't ready. So when you go upstairs, go to the last room on the left. That's room seven like we discussed." I gave MJ a kiss to show her my encouragement.

"Okay, here it goes." Maria said while she slowly walked towards the stairs and then she was gone.

I knew what I was doing. I'd been preparing her for this since we reconnected a few months ago. I could see the yearning in her eyes for the lifestyle and I knew she was willing to do whatever it took to get it. We were a good pair in a lot of ways and the fact that I could trust her with this made me feel like she could really be the one for me.

I made a quick phone call so that the cleaning crew would come back in a couple of hours to clean the house. I didn't want anyone here while Maria was working her magic. Of course I had some people posted up outside just in case things went south. I'm never out here doing this kind of business without my people.

I walked over to the kitchen island, poured some scotch. I turned on the camera that I'd installed in that room. There were seven suitors that I wanted MJ to take down literally one by one. Our business depended on it. And MJ was taking them down alright like a well seasoned porn star. MJ approached the first suitor with a bit of a tease in her walk and followed it up with using her hands and fingers to tickle his body. I could tell he was excited by the way he gazed at her but his dick was limp as fuck as if he suffered from erective dysfunction. MJ knew exactly what to do as she played with his balls and talked dirty to him. She asked him about his fantasies and he told her he wanted to only see her from behind. He was a white man who had a fetish for dark-skinned black women but mentioned he couldn't find the right black woman who would allow him to let it loose like he wanted to.

MJ allowed him to just stare at her from behind and incessantly rub on her and smack her ass. Dude was too geeked and sure enough, his dick started standing up and immediately, MJ grabbed his dick, slid her wet pussy on top of it, and she began hittin' em with the reverse cowgirl. She swayed her hips back and forth with slow motions and then picked up speed when she noticed how excited he was getting. He appeared to be heaven as he was basking in the glistening of her dark skin and roundness of her curves while he held onto her hips for dear life. My mans could barely keep it together. He came in about sixty seconds and the shit went everywhere. He couldn't contain where he shot his nut as it landed all on her back, her ass, and down her thighs. The smile on his face definitely indicated that he was satisfied. All I could think about was how that money would be rolling in very soon.

MJ quickly cleaned herself up and started knocking down each one after that. She gave a dude a six-nine that caused him to squeal, then she straddled the third guy while he spanked her ass profusely. The fourth guy only wanted top-notch head so MJ deepthroated him to the point he started humming because she kept sucking him off while he came. MJ was a fucking G you hear me? Then she signaled to the fifth, sixth, and seventh guys to each stand in a line side by side as she lay down across the bed, opened her legs wide and exposed her wet pussy. She played with herself while they watched. She told them they all had to stoke their own dicks and based on the visual she enjoyed the most, she would choose who would get a taste of her next. One of the guys who looked to be the strongest due to his muscular build, MJ decided to walk over to him and command him to pick her up and fuck her up against the wall. The next guy was ordered to fuck her on the bed while she lied on her stomach. MJ's legs were clenched tightly while he went deep inside her. He looked as if he'd experienced the best orgasm he'd had in a long time as he shook uncontrollably. Then MJ summoned the last guy to bend over a chair while his legs spread apart as she licked his periumum because he liked ass play. She really did that shit. MJ did not come to play. I turned the camera off and knew my work was done. We definitely sealed the deal that night.

We returned to my office the next morning as if it was business as usual. MJ sat across from my desk and we discussed a few final client documents we were awaiting as we prepared to close on a couple of deals.

I gave her excellent feedback per some of the emails I'd received from some of the men who enjoyed her services last night. Due to her exemplary performance, they officially became new multi-million dollar clients of mine which definitely made me extremely happy. I told MJ how much money she would be receiving from this and how much she could potentially make from continuing to work with me. She smiled at me seductively. I told her we would celebrate over wine and dinner tonight but before we did that, she needed to finish me off as I was that fucking excited. She stood up from the other side of my desk, exposing her thick legs in her mini dress, locked my office door and proceeded to thank me.

Pride

My curls were really being unruly today. This is what I get for trying to straighten my hair on my own. I really needed to schedule an appointment with my girl who's the baddest hairstylist in the city. I know she's gonna get me right and return my tresses back to its natural state.

I'd always been adored for my exotic look seeing that my mom is black and my dad is Persian. Growing up though in the hood wasn't exactly the easiest thing for me. The boys loved me but the girls always hated on me like crazy. I'd also developed fast in my pre-teen years so I was not only getting attention from the boys my age but also grown men. I didn't always know how to balance that attention. I also struggled with speaking up for myself because I was a very quiet child much like my paternal grandmother.

She lived in Skokie, a northern suburb of Chicago and I would visit her on the weekends. I would talk to her about school and tell her about how all the boys would flirt with me and tell me about the sexual things they wanted to do with me while the girls would always want to start fights with me because they stayed green with envy. No matter how many times I went through that, it would always catch me off guard when a girl would try to roll up on me. I told my grandmother how I wished I could stop them from hating me. I felt like I always had to fight my way through school and I was tired of it. I could always feel the energy of others around me and I could also tell when another girl's energy was just "off" just by the sight of me.

My grandmother sat me down one day and decided to talk with me about my heritage which included a long history of psychics in our family. She mentioned to me that she'd noticed those psychic abilities becoming more prevalent in me and explained to me how to use my intuitive powers in a beneficial way. I did get a bit beside myself though as I started dabbling in using psychic mind tricks on some of the girls to trip them up. My grandmother forewarned me about that and said that it would bite me in the ass one day and of course it did when I used my abilities to pit two girls against one another so they would take their minds off of fighting me. That fight went down in the history as the most bloodshed at my school. It was brutal and unfortunately, I knew I'd caused it. Needless to say, I never played around with my natural psychic abilities in that way again.

Men always flocked to me. I honestly could get them to do anything I wanted with my looks alone but my aura also captivated men. I didn't really understand the power I had until my late high school years and into college. I didn't even lose my virginity until I was twenty-three years old but after that, it was on and popping. When a friend introduced me to BDSM at a sex party a few years later, I felt like I'd found my tribe. Needless to say, my home that I'd recently renovated a couple of months ago had a beautiful sex room that I furnished myself. I was quite proud of it..

I'd just gotten out of the shower and pinned my hair up so I didn't have to deal with the stringy mess on my head. I put on one of my favorite robes that always made me feel extremely sexy and I sat on the edge of my bed scrolling through my Instagram account when one of my friends called me.

"Hey honey!" I instantly perked up when I answered Grace's call because I wanted to tell her about some finishing touches I'd added to my sex room.

"Yasmin! Girl, what you got going on today? Tiff and Shante' are also on the line as well. I was thinking we could all do brunch in a couple of hours." Grace said as she was always the planner of our friend group.

"Damn, I wish I could go but I decided to switch insurance companies so an inspector is coming out to my house in a few. I mean, I guess it shouldn't take too long but I also need to see if I can squeeze in a quick hair appointment as well." I sighed as I didn't want the inspection and a hair appointment to totally monopolize my day.

"Aiight girl, well if you think you might be able to get out, just let us know. If not, maybe we can go out later tonight for drinks?" Grace asked.

"Okay cool, that might actually work out better anyway. Listen, you all have gotta stop by my house and see my sex room. I just added some finishing touches on it last night. It's so hot. Honestly, I'm feenin' to try it out but then again, I haven't really met any suitable participants if you know what I'm saying?" I chuckled.

"Yasmin girl, you and Grace have always been the sexually adventurous ones in the group. Me and Tiff ain't exactly about that life." Shante' stated with a bit of sarcasm in her voice. "Shiiitt, speak for yourself honey. Me and my man have been kind of playing around with a little bit of kink lately and all I could think to myself is where have I been?" Tiff laughed.

"See that's what I'm talking about!" I cosigned Tiff's statement.

All of a sudden, my dog Anderson started barking like crazy. I began walking downstairs towards my living room to see what was going on. When I looked out of the window, I noticed a car pulling up into my driveway. When the guy got out of the car, I couldn't help but notice how fine he was.

"The insurance guy just pulled up to inspect my home. And let me tell you, he is sexy as hell! I'll have to talk to y'all later." We all said our goodbyes and then I hung up the phone.

When I looked down, I noticed my robe was slightly open and as much as I wanted to greet Mr. Insurance Guy that way, I knew that would appear thirsty as hell so I closed my robe and tied my belt tight. I opened the door before he could ring the bell.

"Hi, excuse me Miss, are you Yasmin?" The insurance guy asked with a slight latin accent. I couldn't help but stare at his muscular arms bulging from his short sleeved shirt revealing a very nice arm sleeve tattoo.

"Yes, I am. And you're Carlos correct?" I asked.

"Yep, that's me. I'll be inspecting the exterior of your home today." Carlos stated while flashing a bright, white smile.

All I could think to myself is that wasn't all I wanted him to inspect but I remained on my best behavior. I could tell though that he was eyeing me a bit as he discreetly looked me up and down. I'm pretty sure he knew there were killer curves underneath my robe. Also, this was the same robe where you could catch a quick view of my pussy print too because my labia naturally poked out a little bit.

"Okay great, well I'll let you do your thing." I said sort of seductively while pulling my door up so the flies wouldn't get inside.

Carlos looked around outside while I watched him from inside my living room. Damn, that man was so sexy. He was so fit and I could imagine him picking me up with ease. I continued to get lost in my thoughts until I realized Carlos was ringing my bell. I walked back over to the door to open it.

"That was pretty quick." I said with a bit of disappointment because I wanted to fantasize a bit longer.

"Oh yeah, these things typically don't take too long." Carlos said.

"Hey, so I just renovated the inside of my house. Do you want to come inside and take a look?" I asked hoping he would say yes.

"Uum, sure. I don't have to but I can take a look and see if you're getting the correct coverage." Carlos looked a bit confused but also curious.

"Okay great. Yep, c'mon in. If you don't mind removing your shoes, that'll be great."

"Sure, no problem." Carlos quickly obliged.

I started giving Carlos a tour of my home. We had to walk through the laundry room to get to the other side but it was dark in there. As I reached for the light, my robe kind of slid up from the bottom and as I felt a draft, I quickly grabbed my robe to pull it back down. Carlos and I locked eyes for a minute and we both kind of laughed a little bit in a sinister kind of way but I quickly returned to giving him the tour of my home.

We began walking upstairs so that he could see the remainder of my home but I forgot to close the door to my sex room.

"Oh, so it looks like you have a bit of a wild side." Carlos smiled.

"You weren't exactly supposed to see that." I started reaching for the door to close it.

Carlos lightly wrapped his hand around my wrist to insinuate I didn't have to do that.

"It's seriously no judgment. I mean, if I can be frank for a minute? You have this sexy robe on. I've been staring at your pussy since you answered the door, and now this sex room. I mean, it looks like you haven't quite broken it in yet. I'd like to try it out if you let me?" Carlos licked his lips while still holding my wrist.

I couldn't get the word *yes* out fast enough. Carlos picked me up with his strong arms and carried me into the room. Then he lifted me up even higher to where my legs were wrapped around his neck and my pussy was staring him right in the face. He started licking me with long, massaging strokes. I was already wet but when he started doing that, I started to feel myself slowly gush and I began to ride his face. I let out an extremely loud moan and my syncopated breaths were aligning to the rhythm of Carlos' tongue licking my clit. But then he began to slow down the pace and switched from holding me up to holding me in his arms as if I was a baby he was trying to soothe.

"Trust me, you won't be disappointed. You're definitely going to cum. I just want to make sure we try out all of the things this room has to offer." Carlos said while walking me over to my spanking bench.

While positioned with my ass in the air, Carlos began to rub my feather whip up and down my back and in between my legs. He lifted the feathers up towards his face and stated how my scent was so erotic and captivating. As much as I wanted to try out all of the different toys and features of my room, I was so ready for Carlos' dick but he was adamant that the focus would be simply on my pleasure.

He laid me down on the bed and used ankle and wrist restraints on me while he pleasured me with a g-spot massager. The way I squirted all over his face and chest was a sight to see. It's one thing to pleasure myself with a vibrator but when someone else is doing it, it just takes it to a whole other level. I just knew Carlos was getting ready to drop his pants but he still had them on even though his shirt was off. Don't get me wrong, I loved how sexy his chest and arms were but I was really starting to wonder when I would get to suck his dick. I was growing impatient at this point.

"Pull out your dick for me or do you want me to beg for it?" I said in my role-playing voice while trying to undo his pants.

"Wait! Don't!" Carlos yelled.

"Uum, did I miss something?" I said with a confused tone.

"Remember, I said this was all about your pleasure." Carlos' voice returned to a calm tone.

"I get that but having your dick inside me would pleasure me." I said softly as I was unsure if he was going to get loud with me again.

"Trust me, there will be plenty of time for that." Carlos tried to reassure me.

It was actually starting to turn me off a bit because it felt like Carlos was hiding something. I was kind of stuck at that point because I no longer wanted to continue. I was just getting a strong sense that something was off but I couldn't quite put my finger on what it was. I mean technically he was a stranger to me so who knows?

"Well, I definitely want to continue this later some time if you're open to doing a lot more exploring?" I stated while trying to hint at the fact that I wanted him to drop his pants next time.

"We can certainly get together again. I do feel like I was just getting started and there's so much more in this room we haven't even begun to play with."

"You're right, but this room isn't going anywhere and I actually want to save some for later." I said seductively even though I was just trying to figure Carlos out.

"Okay, I like that. I'd love to come back later this week if you're available?" Carlos sounded anxious.

"Most definitely." I slid my robe back on and when I stood up, Carlos grabbed a big chunk of my ass stating he couldn't wait to use one of my dildos inside me. Now this shit was definitely giving off some interesting vibes. I'm all for dildos but he wanted to use a dildo on me before he used his own dick? Yeah, not sure about that one.

I walked Carlos back downstairs to the front door. We kissed briefly before he headed to his car. All I could think was this encounter turned into something I wasn't expecting.

* * *

Today was such a long, brutal day at work. While I was thankful for the lifestyle being a realtor afforded me, it was also downright disrespectful at times. It's always a pain when you've gone through such a long process with a buyer and then they decide to back out after the purchase agreement has been signed. All I wanted was a glass of wine and a visit from Carlos. His head game was amazing and I could use a little of that in my life right now.

As I entered my home, I took off my heels at the door, walked over to my sofa, and plopped down with a sigh of exhaustion. I really didn't want to answer any more calls or cook. It definitely looked like it was going to be an UberEats kind of situation tonight.

I felt my phone vibrate next to me and I started not to look to see who was calling but something told me to look anyway. It was Carlos. Even though I was pleasantly surprised, I was also confused by how we really hadn't talked since we met at my house a week ago. There was a bit of phone tag happening between us and his texts always seemed so dry to me which is why I'd rather speak with him over the phone.

"Hello?" I answered.

"Hey Mama, what's good?" Carlos responded casually.

"Uum, well you called me so?" I could tell I was already getting irritated.

"You know, you Boss Babes types are something else. Always so demanding." Carlos chuckled.

"Excuse me? Who do you think you're talking to?" I said with a bit of sass.

"Listen, I know your type. You have something to prove. Especially you mixed girls.

Always trying to overcompensate." Carlos chuckled again.

"So Carlos, I don't know if you're serious right now but you're really skating on thin ice.

You don't know me and stop trying to act like you do."

"Believe me, I know more about you than you think." Carlos said in a secretive tone.

"Okay, let's just do this. Just forget we even met. I really don't have time for this right now. I've had a long day. I have a lot on my plate. Either you're going to be available to relax me or you really can just step the fuck off." I said angrily.

"I knew that side of you would come out soon. Like I said, I can tell your type. Sexy and shit on the outside but just pure evil on the inside. But it's all good. I'm glad I got a chance to see your little sex room though." Carlos said sarcastically.

"And like I said, just step the fuck off with your little dick ass." Even though I'd never seen his dick, I found myself always resorting to saying that in an argument with a man. I know saying that was typically a huge hit to a man's ego, but Carlos deserved it at this point. He was acting really crazy like he knew me for some reason.

"What the fuck did you say to me bitch?" Carlos yelled.

I immediately hung up on him and blocked his number. That was also a very weird phone call. Why was he being so aggressive? What did I ever do to that man? I didn't even know him. Shit, that's what I get with my horny ass and then inviting him into my home. I'm definitely not doing anything like that again.

I called my friend Grace to tell her what happened. She was always the voice of reason for me. When I told her about Carlos the day he and I had sex, she said I really shouldn't have let him into my home seeing that he was only inspecting the outside and now I'm starting to think she was right.

I found myself dozing off and before I knew it, I had been asleep for four hours! When I woke up, it was about one o'clock in the morning so I grabbed my heels by the front door and started walking up to my bedroom. I was literally peeling off my clothes while walking up the stairs. I took a long hot shower, towel dried my hair, threw on a robe and slipped right into bed. I commanded

Siri to turn off all of the lights in my home but then I heard a sound, like a thump. I sat up in my bed attempting to not make a sound to see if I heard it again. All of a sudden, Anderson started barking constantly. I grabbed my gun out of the nightstand and slowly walked downstairs. I would be a fool to think living alone without protection was smart so I was definitely prepared.

By the time I got to the foot of the stairs, Anderson stopped barking but he was still positioned at the back door as if he saw something. I was thoroughly convinced someone had probably been snooping around the outside of my house. Anderson was a guard dog, a German Shepherd to be exact so this was no coincidence. Someone had been back there. I was exhausted but I still decided to check the camera footage from the rear of my home. Surprisingly, I saw no one on the camera within the last hour which was strange.

I slowly walked back upstairs but I was a little on edge. I know someone was back there.

I couldn't shake that feeling as I attempted to doze back off to sleep.

* * *

"Girl, I didn't know it was going to be this crowded tonight." Grace yelled while sipping her drink.

"Yeah, me too. Quite honestly, I'm over these networking mixers but let's just stay for another ten to fifteen minutes and leave. Maybe we can go and listen to some live music somewhere." I said while scanning the room.

We were attending yet another real estate networking event, but I was over it and ready to go.

"What's wrong? You keep looking around like you're spooked about something?" Grace questioned.

"Well, about a month ago, Anderson was barking like crazy one night and I think someone was outside my home but no one ever appeared on the camera footage. It just kind of shook me up a bit. And then I've been having this weird feeling like I'm being followed or something." I said while still scanning the room.

"Seriously?" Why didn't you tell me?

"I don't know. Maybe because nothing else happened but it just seems weird." I said with a disappointed tone because I couldn't quite figure out what was going on.

"Wait a minute. When did you meet that guy Carlos? Grace inquired.

"About a month ago. Why?"

"Did you meet him before this happened or after?" Grace asked as if she was morphing into Nancy Drew.

"Wait a minute, do you think he's somehow connected to how I'm feeling?"

"I mean, think about it. You haven't had this feeling before. You said you think someone might have been outside your home. He's been to your home and he's aware that you have cameras and a guard dog. All I'm saying is you said he acted extremely weird, aggressive, and a bit arrogant. I just wouldn't put it past him." Grace said while trying to connect the dots.

Grace really got me thinking but just when I was about to ask her a question another realtor walked up to her and they began talking. I got lost in my thoughts and forgot anyone else was in the room.

"Yasmin!" Grace yelled.

"Oh my God, what?" I yelled back.

"I called your name like three times. Clearly you were somewhere else in your mind."

Grace seemed frustrated.

"Well, it's kind of hard not to be fixated on my thoughts after you planted all of those things in my head." I said in a similar frustrated tone.

"I was trying to introduce you to Stacy. She's with Birkman Properties. She moved here from Texas almost a year ago. I invited her out tonight so she could get more acclimated to the Chicago scene." Grace said while trying to make the introduction.

"Well, as far as the Chicago scene, I've actually been laying kind of low for the last few months after a situation I had with an insurance guy I met at a homebuyers workshop back in February." Stacy said.

Stacy was a pretty petite woman, about five foot three. She seemed to be a bit timid but again, she was still adjusting to life in Chicago so maybe that's why I was picking up on that particular vibe.

"What are you talking about? What insurance guy at a homebuyers workshop? Yasmin and I are well connected in Chicago real estate so we probably know him." Grace asked.

"His name is Carlos." Stacy whispered as if she was telling a secret.

"Wait a minute. Did you say Carlos? As in a Dominican guy with big arms?" I nervously asked.

"Yep, that's him." Stacy said while looking me directly in my eyes.

"So can you tell us the situation you had with Carlos?" Grace asked while appearing to revert back to her detective ways.

"Again, being new to Chicago, I was meeting people left and right but I met Carlos at a homebuyers workshop that I was assisting with. We made small talk, flirted a bit, and then he asked me out for a drink afterwards. We actually talked for hours. Or should I say I did most of the talking. He said the focus should be on me as he expressed he's not the type to make everything about himself. I was drawn to him because of that. We went on a few more dates and then well, we finally started messing around. That's when things started to change. I saw more of an arrogant and domineering side of him. He was also very demanding sexually. He wanted our sexual encounters to go his way all the time. He was great at pleasing me orally but it took forever for us to actually have intercourse. He kept telling me we would get there because he said he wanted to make sure that I was extremely pleased as a woman first.

When I finally saw his dick, I couldn't believe it! He had a micropenis. I just couldn't understand how this sexy, muscular, yet arrogant man really didn't shit down there." Stacy barely took a breath while trying to continue the story. It's as if she had been waiting to get this off of her chest.

It started making sense too as to why he didn't want to take off his pants when I asked him to. For a minute, I actually felt bad for him.

"So what happened after that?" I asked.

"I couldn't say anything. I was just stuck because I couldn't believe how small it was. So I made up some lie about having to head back home because I had a lot of showings the next day or something. But I could tell that he knew I was no longer interested. So I began ghosting him and I didn't return any of his calls. Plus his behavior was starting to change anyway and I no longer felt comfortable around him. But then weird things started happening like noises outside of my home. I kept seeing this red Dodge Charger when I would be heading out at night, whether driving down my block or at events I was attending, and I just always felt like someone was watching me. I called a good friend of mine who's a psychic and I had a reading." Stacy continued.

At this point my heart started racing as soon as she said she met with a psychic because I felt like I already knew what she was going to say. My own psychic abilities were kicking in high gear at this point.

"When I sat down for my reading, she positioned some tarot cards in front of me and asked me to pull three. All I remember is seeing swords and chariots. She mentioned someone was following me and that I needed to get away from a particular man who was dangerous. Then my psychic friend flipped a card and said he put a tracking device in my car."

The glass of wine I was holding slipped out of my hand and shattered on the floor. Grace and I locked eyes as we knew right then I was in some serious trouble.

Envy

Darius Charles, better known as DC, was a sports agent to celebrities but also a hard money lender. When it comes to hard money lenders, I can't lie, they're pretty grimy. These loans are typically short term and non-confirming for commercial and investment properties. If a loan or mortgage application has been denied or if you're just trying to avoid the lengthy process of getting approved for a loan through the traditional route, then you might try your hand at a hard money lender. That comes with a price though; such as a higher interest rate, a larger down payment, riskier financing, and/or shorter repayment terms. So basically, it's like a payday loan for properties and it ain't pretty. I've worked with DC on several occasions and even though he's such a sweetheart, his business practices were questionable at best.

DC and James were the best of friends which is how I'd come to know DC and appreciate him. We'd had a brother/sister kind of bond for the longest and I managed his portfolio of over one hundred properties so there was definitely a level of trust between us. DC is also married to a tax consultant named Chanel. Chanel and I also had a pretty cool relationship until I noticed her eyeing me kind of hard one day when James and I were hanging out with them at their house in Barrington. When I told James it seemed like

Chanel was looking at me a bit seductively and I didn't know why, he mentioned to me that Chanel was indeed bi-sexual and even though she was married to DC, she never hid her salacious appetite for women. Of course DC had no problem with it because he would get the opportunity to partake as well when she would bring other women around. But after the Frank Breezy and Arianna fiasco, I had my fair share of being someone's third and I was not interested.

Don't get me wrong, DC was a very beautiful man. He was about six foot three with very smooth, dark chocolate skin. His hair was thick enough to still sport some 360 waves and he always kept a clean goatee. He was strong and built like a security guard which I'm pretty sure worked to his advantage to ensure that people paid him on time. But again, he and James were the closest of friends so it never crossed my mind to even think about him in that way until I received a text from him that completely caught me off guard.

Hey MJ, check your account right quick. I just sent you something through Zelle.

The text that I'd just received from DC was a bit odd. Typically, this was not how we did business so I couldn't quite grasp why he wanted me to check my account. When I logged in, to my surprise, DC had sent me ten thousand dollars.

DC, what the hell is this for? I texted him back.

The three dots appeared on my phone screen as I was waiting for his response with anticipation because none of this made sense.

I'm heading to Jamaica in a couple days and I want you to come with me.

Okay, now my heart was beginning to race because this definitely didn't seem like it was business related.

You can't be serious. I texted him back.

Dead ass. Please no questions. I can't make any reservations for you on my account for obvious reasons but I want you to book a first class flight to Montego Bay. I'll pick you up from the airport and we'll head to the villa together. The rest of the money in your account will be for you to splurge on whatever you want when you arrive. Again, no questions. I'll explain everything when you get there.

Okay, there was nothing else to make of this besides this being a very luxurious dick appointment and honestly, I was a bit curious to see what this was all about. I mean James and I were kicking it pretty heavy but hell, I was still in a bit of a hoe phase right now and it wasn't like James had officially locked me down. I know DC and James were friends but if DC was putting all this together, I'm pretty sure he knew how to move in a manner that would be low key. But damn, he just dropped ten thousand dollars in my bank account like that? Ooh, that's so fucking sexy and I couldn't wait to see what was in store.

* * *

It was about one-thirty in the afternoon when I arrived at the airport in Montego Bay. I'd literally received a text from James and DC at the same time. James was reminding me of an upcoming meeting he and I were scheduled for early next week which I disregarded and the text from DC was him letting me know a car was waiting for me out front. I thought he was going to meet me at the airport but he later mentioned that he would be waiting for me at the villa.

I chose to ignore James' text because we got into an argument the day before I left to go to Jamaica. I kind of started that argument on purpose so he would think I wasn't talking to him for a few days so that I could pop out right quick with DC and he wouldn't have a clue as to what was going on. Okay, I know that seemed a bit trifling but he had no rights to me especially with all the women he was still fucking anyway.

I secured my luggage and made my way to the exit to meet up with my driver. I was greeted by a gorgeous Jamaican man who opened my door to an exquisite drop top silver Porsche. I could already tell I was in for a treat, but the question still remained as to why now? I guess I should just focus on fuck now and ask questions later. The drive to the villa was perfect. The wind blowing in my hair and the sun on my skin felt amazing. It was so good to break out of the Chicago weather for a bit and enjoy the island. The sounds of Reggae music, the white sandy beaches, and being greeted by some of the most beautiful smiles was just what I needed to break away from the daily grind of real estate.

When we pulled up to the villa, DC walked outside towards the car in some relaxed white linen pants, with no shirt on exposing his glistening dark skin, and visible tattoos. I was definitely pleased with his dick print as well.

"I've been waiting for that smile all day." DC said while helping me out of the car.

DC told my driver that he appreciated his services and that he had it from here. I noticed he tipped the driver three hundred dollars with ease and gave him a pat on the back and sent him on his way.

"So what is this all about?" I asked curiously.

"We'll have plenty of time to chat once I get you settled." DC said mysteriously.

I was extremely intrigued and horny at the same time. This was also a bit weird considering our business relationship as well as our personal connection because of James.

As soon as I walked in the door of the villa, I was stunned by how beautiful it was. It was a four bedroom river house that exuded the finest detail. There was also a chef in the kitchen already preparing food for us.

"Wow DC, this is amazing!" I said excitedly.

"I'm so glad you were able to make it MJ." DC lightly grabbed my hand and kissed it while looking very intently in my eyes.

DC signaled for the maid to carry my bags into the master bedroom. We sat on one of the sofas while the chef continued to prepare lunch for us.

"So, you've kept me in suspense long enough. What is this all about?" I asked.

"I'm pretty sure you can grasp that I'm a man of action. You'll be here for a couple of days so we'll have plenty of time to talk." DC said while moving in closer to me on the sofa and lightly rubbing my thigh while we both locked eyes.

"Yeah, so I'm not sure why we're still sitting here then." I said while licking my lips.

"Damn." DC said while grabbing my hand and guiding me to our room. I looked back and noticed the chef had a half smile on his face almost as if he was wishing he was in DC's position right now.

DC was so Chicago because as soon as we walked into our room, I heard R. Kelly softly playing on the speaker. You can take the nigga out of Chicago but you can't take the Chicago out of the nigga. DC sat on the chaise lounge at the edge of the bed and moved an end table in front of him so that he could begin rolling up his weed. He poured some Hennessy in a mug along with a honey pack and mixed it with his finger. DC was turning me on so much that I immediately walked over to him and started tonguing him down while he grabbed my ass.

"See, that's what I'm talking about. I could tell how that sundress was hugging you that you didn't have on any panties." DC said in between kisses.

"Listen, I stay ready so I ain't gotta get ready. I'm still not sure what this is all about but I do know I'm about to get some dick." I said and then continued kissing DC.

We both stood up and continued to tongue kiss. I pushed him down on the bed and noticed his dick was hard as a rock. The wet spots from his pre-cum were very visible in his white linen pants. When I pulled his pants down, my mouth started salivating and I began giving him some serious head like my life depended on it. DC's dirty talk was top tier because I became more sloppy with it the more he talked his shit. I knew if I kept going at that rate, I would make him cum and it was just too soon for that. I needed every inch of his big, black, hard dick inside my wet pussy. I licked his balls while stroking his dick and then I decided to sit on him.

I almost couldn't contain myself. It felt so good. The way he grabbed my hips as I swayed side to side as if we had been together like this before. I still couldn't believe I was doing this but I didn't care because the shit was so good. He gave my titties some serious love as well. I needed that so much. I couldn't stand when men ignored the twins. The way he sucked my nipples while grabbing my ass was just right. I already knew I would need some of this from time to time once we returned back to the States.

"Hmmm, MJ, you feel so fucking good. Damn, your pussy is so wet. You must've been waiting on me." DC said while I continued to ride him.

Before I knew it, DC had switched positions to where he was on top of me, missionary style while he continued to go deeper into my pussy. He then began gazing into my eyes. I wasn't exactly expecting this level of intimacy but clearly we were here.

"Damn, DC you ain't playing no games." I said while moaning.

"I'm definitely not. I wanted to take you into the shower, but as soon as you pushed me on the bed, I couldn't wait any longer." DC said in between strokes.

"We can still get in the shower later. I'm pretty sure you can handle a second round right?" I asked curiously.

"Hell yeah! Looking forward to it. You don't know how long I've been wanting you."

DC said while kissing my forehead and fucking me at the same time.

"Uum, what do you mean?" I asked while moaning still.

"I know that nigga James ain't the one for you. I've been wanting you since I met you. James ain't shit. You really should be mine." DC said while we were still having sex which became kind of weird.

"DC, wait what? I put my hands on DC's shoulder indicating that I wanted him to stop.

"Babe, chill, I'm just playing with you. You feel so good. Sometimes a nigga just be saying shit. Don't take it seriously. When the pussy is this good, I'm liable to say anything."

"Oh okay." I said confusingly.

Even though DC kind of threw me off for a minute, the dick was so good that I just let him carry on without thinking twice about what he said. I'm glad that I continued on because he gave me multiple orgasms out of this world.

"I can tell you enjoyed every bit of this dick."

"I sure did and I want some more. You really didn't need that honey pack that you asked me to bring." I said while DC was still in between my thighs.

"How about we enjoy some of that food my chef hooked up, then we can get right back at it? Plus, I need to see your fat ass walk. Damn, your pussy is so good."

I got out of bed and pranced around the room to honor DC's request. We didn't quite stick to our plans of eating right away. We fucked one more time and that shit was amazing.

* * *

I miss Jamaica already. I wish I could've stayed longer but I had some business to tend to back home but a couple days in the islands was more than enough time to get my entire back blown out. DC really did make that quick baecation a fun one. I still kind of wondered though why he said he felt like James wasn't the one for me. I know he said he was playing but that's still kind of a weird thing to say. I mean, there are times where I even question my relationship with James because we're not always on the same page, but why would DC say that?

I'm loud and much of an open book. I guess you can say James is discreet but really what I think he wants is for me to be a secret. He's probably doing that so he can have other bitches thinking he's so available. I don't know and I don't care which is why I will be in my hoe phase for as long as I want. I'm just a "what you see is what you get" kind of person. I ain't frontin' for nobody; but James is all about appearances. That shit be getting on my nerves which is why I don't regret meeting up with DC.

DC and I had a talk before I left Jamaica about our little rendezvous staying with us and that no one needed to know including his wife. The thought came to me though that she might be more upset that she couldn't join in the action.

I'd just gotten back home from my trip a couple of days ago and I immediately got back to work. I was so tired, I barely slept in my bed and mainly slept in the guest room downstairs. When I walked upstairs to my bedroom, all of my paperwork and files were still scattered across my bed just where I'd left them before going out of town. Uugh, I really need to get more organized but that was the last thing on my mind when I was getting ready to see DC. I also needed to call James before he started blowing up my phone.

I stared at James' number in my contacts trying to gather my thoughts before calling him. I didn't want him to suspect anything different in the tone of my voice. I didn't need him fishing for anything. The last thing I was trying to do was come in between friends.

"So are you finally done with your tantrum?" James answered my call without even saying hello.

"See, this is why you get on my nerves. You don't take me seriously."

"MJ, please. Give me something to be serious about. You be having your little attitude when stuff don't go your way. I ain't got time for that shit. So, I give you your space until you figure whoever the hell you wanna be that day. Sometimes I get the business MJ, the vixen MJ, or the emotional MJ. I can't concern myself with that. But anyway, I'm glad you called because I just pulled up in front of your house. Grab your stuff and come out. I'm taking you out to eat."

"Uum, how do you know I ain't got plans?" I said with a bit of sass.

"Quit playing and come get in this car."James said sternly.

As much as James would get underneath my skin at times, I loved that he was an alpha male. He always took charge but sometimes, I still needed him to be a bit soft with me. I don't know how many times I've had to remind him to talk to me like a woman and not like one of his male colleagues but then when I say that, he's always got some excuse for how he wasn't raised that way, blah, blah, blah. Anyway, I wasn't going to miss out on a good meal. Fine dining was James' specialty.

"Okay babe, I'm coming, damn. I just need to freshen up a bit. You can either stay your ass in the car or come in."

"You know if I come in, imma have your ass laid across the bed. And right now we've got some business to discuss. So like I said, just come on."

Uugh, dammit. I was actually still kind of tired from my trip but I didn't need James thinking something else was going on so I took a quick hoe bath, changed into something a little more sexy because James absolutely hated to see me in sweats and a t-shirt, and made my way out of the door.

* * *

"Babe, I thought we were going out to eat." I said while my stomach was growling.

"We can still eat here. I just wanted to stop by my guy's new cigar lounge because I didn't get a chance to make it to his grand opening. Babe, just order some wings or something for now and then we'll head downtown later." James said while eyeing some chick at the bar.

"Are you serious right now? I got dressed up for this? And who is that bitch you're smiling at over there?" I was getting increasingly frustrated.

"It doesn't matter where we go. When we're out together, I always appreciate you looking your best. C'mon now, you're a representation of me. And the woman at the bar is my guy's old lady so don't trip." James seemed to be exhausted with me.

"What do you mean I'm a representation of you? You don't fully have me sir. Don't get it twisted."

"MJ, stop talking slick. You know you're my woman. I waited on YOU remember? Girl, chill." James said while lighting up a cigar.

All I could think about was, I put on my nice wig and dress only to have it overpowered by cigar smoke.

"Anyway, I'm going to the bathroom."

When I was walking towards the ladies room, I noticed all of the men staring at me as usual but towards the back entrance of the lounge, I thought I saw DC. I started getting a bit nervous because I wasn't quite ready for all of us to be in the same space just yet. I didn't feel like I could quite play off the fact that he and I just slept together a few days ago. I really needed to feel DC out one more time so I decided to go out of the back door to see if I could catch up to him but he was nowhere to be found. It was strange that of all the places, he ended up here tonight. Oh well, maybe it wasn't him.

I walked in the ladies room, washed my hands and applied another stroke of lip gloss to my lips. I must admit the dj was hitting in this place as I started moving my body to the sounds of some trap music. Even though I was looking forward to dining at a fancy restaurant, I was no stranger to a little ratchetness because it's all about balance.

When I walked out of the restroom, I seriously thought I saw DC again in my peripheral view so I did a double take and walked to the back entrance again to see if that was him. Like before, he wasn't in sight. I know I'm not losing it or even remotely worried about the situation. Why would I be? I can't imagine DC willing to risk it all and blow up his marriage along with his friendship with James.

I walked back to the table where James and I were sitting but he was conversing with some men at another table. They were laughing and consistently puffing on their cigars. I know we better not spend the entire night here. I could've stayed home for this.

"Hey pretty lady." A tall, dark and handsome brother said to me while I was taking a sip of my cognac.

"Good evening." I smiled back.

"By any chance is this seat taken?"

"Uum, yes it is." James said while seemingly appearing out of nowhere.

"Oh, my bad. I didn't know that was you. No disrespect." The mystery man stated while walking away.

"Damn, I can't even be gone for a second MJ before someone tries to scoop you up."

James chuckled.

"Well, can you blame these men? I'm coming up in here looking damn good. You're the only one that doesn't seem to notice." I said with an attitude.

"There you go again. Women always be needing so much attention. You know I'm locked in to you. As a matter of fact, we need to really talk about solidifying our relationship." James casually said while puffing on his cigar.

"What do you mean by that?"

"Like I said, solidifying what we have. We're doing everything together already. We do business together, we fuck, and peple know you're my lady. I want us to get married."

"James, what the hell? Is this supposed to be a proposal?" I said in a confused tone.

"Look, I'm not into all that proposal stuff. I know what I want and it's you. You're killing it in real estate and you're going to get bigger and better. A lot of that has to do with me grooming you of course. We would be such a force together."

"I don't know if I'm ready for all of that right now."

"I really don't understand what there is to think about but just like before, I'll wait because you're worth it."

Even though I would've appreciated a real proposal, it did make me feel good that James wanted a future with me, but what would that future look like? I mean, would I still be bending over for his big-time clients or am I just his hoe right now because we aren't married? He definitely couldn't find out about DC now.

"Yo! What up DC?" James yelled across the room.

I was looking down at the time when James noticed him. I was hoping my face didn't look like I saw a ghost but in a sense, I felt like I did because I could've sworn I saw DC not too long ago by the restroom. This shit was really starting to get weird.

James and DC gave each other the kind of brotherly hug that only close friends give to one another. It was just a reminder of how close they really were.

"Hey MJ, how are you beautiful?" DC stretched his arms out and gave me a hug as well. He called every woman beautiful so it made no sense for him to switch up now just because all three of us were together. That would've made things look even more suspicious.

"I'm good. Didn't expect to see you here." I said nervously.

"Yeah man, I definitely didn't expect to see you on this side of town tonight. I thought you would've still been in Jamaica." James asked.

Shit, so James knew DC went to Jamaica. So clearly they talked about his trip but by the looks of it, James still didn't even know I'd gone out of town.

"Man, I got back a few days ago. I miss it though. It's always nice out there, but this time was definitely special." DC said while quickly taking a glimpse at me.

"That's what's up. Did Chanel end up going with you?" James sure was asking a lot of questions.

"Naw man, she couldn't make it this time. But like I said, I still had a great time. Closed a deal while I was out there, enjoyed the sun, and I still had a little fun out there if you know what I mean?" DC chuckled.

"Yeah man, I know how you and Chanel get down seeing that she loves the ladies too but shit, I know she be trippin' if you getting a little action without her."

"Believe it or not, she's been cool. As long as she know who I'm fucking around with, she straight." DC said calmly.

Wait a minute, did Chanel know it was me? I wanted to ask so badly.

"You still kicking it with your assistant? James asked while sipping some cognac.

"Yeah, something like that." James and DC laughed while clearly having some male bonding time. Thankfully, I didn't come up in the conversation but I was still convinced that DC had something up his sleeve.

"Hey babe, I'm gonna grab another drink. Did you all want anything?" I asked.

"Naw babe, I'm good for now." James stated.

"Actually, I'm going to check in with the bartender anyway. I need to chop it up with her so I'll go with you." DC said casually.

DC and I walked over to the bar together and there was a bit of awkward silence until I broke the ice.

"DC, uum what's going on? I know I saw you by the back door earlier." I said sternly.

"Girl, what are you talking 'bout?" DC said coyly.

"Stop fucking with me DC. I'm serious." I whispered aggressively.

"Aiight, so yeah I pulled up at your spot earlier and noticed James' car so I followed ya'll. Look, I told you James ain't for you." DC looked at me seriously.

"Wait one damn minute. You said you were just talking shit because we were fucking. So you really meant that shit?"

"Look, don't get all extra right now or James is gonna see us talking over here like this. Just think about what I said. I know you and James doing your thing but I know how that motherfucker is pimping you out and that shit ain't cool. You don't ever have to do that with me. You're still going to be a boss in your own right, still make a ton of money, and live the good life. I'll give you whatever you want."

"DC, you can't be serious right now. Okay, so let's say hypothetically you are, what about Chanel?"

"I'm actually working on divorcing her. She just doesn't know it yet."

"I can't believe I'm listening to this bullshit right now. Listen, I'm in a hoe phase. We had some fun and I'm even game for having some more fun but I ain't trying to blow up neither one of our spots right now."

"MJ, I ain't going down without a fight. I haven't been able to stop thinking about you since Jamaica. Hell, I was thinking about you even before Jamaica. I'm just into you; everything from the smell of your hair, your walk, your voice, that wet pussy...."

"Shhh, don't be saying that shit out loud right now."

"All I'm saying is, I want and need you in my life. James really doesn't deserve you." "You said that before, what do you mean?" I asked inquisitively.

"Let's just say this. If ya'll really get together, you just might want to watch your back. James just cares about money and he'll do whatever and use whoever to get it."

I wonder if this conversation had anything to do with James asking me to marry him. Is that why he wants to "so-call" solidify our relationship so he could get my money too? I couldn't believe this shit!

"Whatever you're talking about right now, just drop it. Pretend like this conversation never happened. As a matter of fact, just forget Jamaica ever happened. Clearly, we are not in a space to have a decent friends with benefits kind of situation. Let's just go back to getting this money. I'll connect with you tomorrow about that crazy tenant we were talking about the other day."

I started to walk back to the table James and I were sitting at until DC grabbed my arm.

"MJ, I know you're feeling some kind of way because of what I said about James but don't ever say Jamaica didn't happen. That shit was amazing and you know it was. Listen, I ain't gon' bug you about all of this. I'll give you some space and keep it business for now but like I said, I want you and I believe I will have you."

I rolled my eyes at DC, grabbed my drink and walked off.

* * *

I couldn't believe the conversation DC and I had the other night. I was still pissed off by that and there was no avoiding him because our work lives were so intertwined. For instance, today was a typical work day of doing property management for DC including a mountain of shit such as viewing properties, serving five-day notices, attending court dates, and reviewing repair requests.

I was actually planning on heading over to James' office this morning but when he told me DC was stopping by, I made up some stupid excuse to keep from running into both of them at the same time. I just didn't feel like it today. After organizing some files in my office, I decided to head over to one of DC's properties because I needed to follow up with some irate tenants whose toilets were backing up yesterday and running over. I ended up turning the water off in the building so the tenants were seriously blowing my phone up all morning. When I stopped by for a property inspection, I noticed there was a greasy substance on the basement floor which led to me finding out that the plumbing was backed up in the entire building. I tell you, when it rains it pours.

Now DC is calling on my bat phone which is my other property management phone. As much as I didn't want to talk to him right now, I needed to keep in the loop regarding what was happening at one of his properties so I answered his call.

"Hello, this is MJ." I said in my professional phone voice.

"Damn, you always sound so sexy. You make me wanna——"

"Cut the Usher talk right now. You need to know about what's going on over here." I said sternly.

"Okay babe, calm down. Where are you?"

"I'm not your babe so don't call me that. Listen, I know I sent you the invoice about the backed up toilets yesterday but I found some greasy shit all on the basement floor this morning and now plumbing is backed up in the entire fucking building."

"Alright, I hear you and of course all this shit will be taken care of. I know it's fucked up but hey, it's the name of the game. You sound extremely frustrated right now." DC stated in a concerned tone.

"Well, DC there's just a lot going on right now and my day really just started. I have so much other stuff to do. I'm just stressed."

"I hear you loud and clear and quite honestly, I don't like to hear you stressing out like this."

I heard chatter in the background as if DC was around a lot of people and then I heard James' voice!

"Are you still at James' office? Are you out of your fucking mind talking to me like this around him?" I felt myself growing more frustrated and upset.

"MJ, c'mon now. Yeah, I'm at his office but I'm down the hall. The nigga's voice just carries. He's not even close by. Look, I'll let you handle your business but catch up with me later this evening, I want to talk to you about something."

"DC, what did I tell you before? Unless it's about business, we have nothing to talk about. I'll keep you posted on your other properties later today."

I hung up the phone, looked down at my shoes and noticed grease on my $700 heels, but I didn't even care. James funds my work wardrobe anyway.

I started walking up to the third floor while wiping my heels on the carpet along the way. I knocked on one of the tenants' doors. They didn't answer right away but I knew they were there because the smell of weed greeted me before I even reached their unit.

"Yeah, who is it?" The tenant loudly asked from the inside.

"It's MJ." I screamed back.

The tenant opened the door with her bonnet on, most of her shirt unbuttoned clearly looking disheveled as if she'd just finished having some straight bustdown sex. I noticed her boyfriend sitting on the couch rolling up a blunt while the rest of their apartment looked like they just didn't give a fuck. This shit was so ghetto.

"Damn, it took you long enough. Can you all finally fix this motherfucking toilet?" The tenant asked nonchalantly while her sagging titties practically hung down to her exposed fupa.

"Listen, I just came to deliver this five-day notice. I will have to put you out if you don't pay your rent by the first."

"You got a lot of fucking nerve coming over here talkin' 'bout some rent due and this toilet been fucked up for the longest." The tenant said in between puffing her weed.

I wasn't even wasting my time with this woman. I was licensed to carry and I definitely carried my piece when coming over to this building. My hope was that I never had to use it but I would if I needed to.

"Look, I already said what I said. The notice is on the table. Either pay the rent or you'll be packing up and leaving sweetheart. Have a nice day."

I walked towards the door and let myself out. I heard the woman call me a bitch from inside her unit as I was walking down the hall. I didn't care. I had too much other stuff on my plate. After I left the property and got in my car, James started calling me.

"Hey babe, what's up?" I answered while going over my to-do list on my lap.

"You sound preoccupied." James said.

"Nothing out of the ordinary, just the typical busy day. What's up?"

"DC was just here at the office. He was telling me you had some shit go down with plumbing and serving five-day notices. You good?"

"Yeah babe, I'm good. Nothing I can't handle."

"Okay, well, I know you're busy. But later this evening around six o'clock, can you stop by my office?"

"Sure, what's going on?"

"Just stop by. I have a few things I need to do too but I'll be back around five forty-five this evening. I'll explain when you get here." James said cryptically.

"Okay, will it just be us? Will DC still be there?"

"It'll just be us. Why did you ask about DC?"

I could tell I slipped up and I felt like I could hear it in James' voice that he was reading more into my question so I tried to clean it up.

"Nothing babe. I just asked because you know how we get down in your office and I'm kind of needing some dick anyway. I just wanted to make sure there were no distractions."

I really tried to sound convincing.

"Oh okay, well you know I always got you on that. But yep, just bring your fine ass over here later. I'll make sure you're good and satisfied."

"Okay babe, I'll see you later."

I hung up the phone but for some reason, James sounded a little different as if he had something else on his mind. He just didn't sound like himself. Hopefully he was okay. Unfortunately, I couldn't spend a lot of time thinking about that right now because I had so much work to do and so many places to be. I started my car and my bluetooth immediately started blasting Mary J. Blige's "Just Fine." I sped off and made my way to court.

* * *

I pulled up right next to James' car in front of his office. The lot was definitely empty as it looked as if many other people in the neighboring offices were done for the day as well. I still wasn't sure if James was doing okay so I decided to pick up a veggie wrap and a green tea for him just in case he hadn't eaten yet. James had been going pretty hard in the gym lately and said he wanted to be more health conscious so I thought it would be a nice gesture.

When I got to the door, James smiled at me and let me in. He gave me a really warm embrace, unlike the usual ass grab greeting. He then kissed me on my forehead.

I walked over to the sofa in the lobby, placed his food on the table and proceeded to try to tongue him down but he stopped me.

"Babe, are you okay?" I asked confusingly.

"Yeah babe, I'm good. It's just been a long day. Is this for me?" James picked up the bag of food.

"Yep, I figured you probably hadn't eaten since this morning so I grabbed you something."

"You're such a fast learner." James chuckled.

"Well, I know what else you like." I said seductively while attempting to unzip James' pants.

"Hold up for a minute. How was your day?" James asked while moving my hands away from his pants and positioning me to sit on the sofa.

It was abnormally quiet in the office. Usually, if no one is there but James, he would still be playing some old school R&B music in the background or something. But that wasn't the case this time. I actually heard the waterfall behind the receptionist's desk loud and clear this time. Don't get me wrong, it was very relaxing and soothing after a long day but usually we fuck first and then he asks me how my day was later.

"I mean, my day was pretty much hell on wheels but I'm okay." I said while crossing my legs trying to reenact the infamous scene from the movie, Indecent Proposal attempting to turn James on.

"That's it? You're not going to go into detail about DC's property?" James asked.

"I mean, there isn't much to tell. There was a major plumbing issue and I had to serve one of the tenants a five-day notice but it wasn't the end of the world. It was just annoying as fuck and I got a little grease on my shoes, but that's it. You seem like you want to ask something else."

My heart was starting to race a bit because this conversation was starting to feel like it was headed in a direction I didn't want it to go.

"I just figured you were really stressed out because DC was here earlier and I heard him say your name on the phone as if he was trying to calm you down. I just thought it was kind of strange. For some reason, the conversation just seemed a bit more intense." James asked while taking a bite out of his wrap and staring at me intently at the same time.

"You know how I get when I'm initially upset. I get a bit loud, but I usually calm down rather quickly. I'm over it now. It's not really a big deal."

"It's funny you say that because last night at the cigar lounge when you went to the bar to get a drink and DC was at the bar with you, it appeared as if you all were having a pretty intense conversation there too but you seemed fine when you came back to our table."

James was really hitting me with his observations and I was starting to feel like the wall was closing in on me.

"Right, I was just mentioning to him about the invoice I'd sent him regarding the toilets backing up and the tenants being frustrated. I didn't mean to worry you. That was just business."

I tried softening my tone a bit so James wouldn't suspect anything.

"So MJ, I'm pretty direct. I'm not the one to beat around no fucking bush."

Oh shit, he's back to calling me MJ and not babe. Yeah, something is going on, I thought to myself.

"Okay, I never expect you to beat around the bush. What are you talking about?" I was really getting nervous at this point.

"You know I want you to be mine. I have no doubt about that. We just work so well together and I was talking to DC earlier today about wanting to do the proper proposal with you because I know you weren't feeling the shit I was talking last night. Plus, I know women. Y'all need that whole down on bended knee with Brian McKinght singing in the background and shit so I was ready to do all that."

I could tell James' mood was becoming a bit more dark and almost cold as he continued to speak and my heart started racing even faster.

"You said *was,* as if you no longer feel that way."

"I was telling DC I wanted to marry you 'cause you know that's my guy. We've been close for a long time. I trust him but some shit has changed."

"Babe, I'm lost. What are you talking about?"

"DC been my boy forever. He's one of those niggas that always keep it one hundred with me but as soon as I started telling him I wanted to marry you, his whole vibe changed. Then he started asking me if I thought marrying you was a good idea. I'm looking like what the fuck? I wasn't asking him for his advice on marrying you. I just wanted him to be the first to know and then ask him to have Chanel do all that fancy shit so I could put together something nice and surprise you but he starts questioning me about my decision. Of course I give him the look like who the fuck you think you talking to and he proceeds to say some shit about how I shouldn't rush into this with you."

"So you don't think he's just being a good friend and just looking out for you? I don't see the problem with that."

"And that's my point. You don't take offense to him saying that? The three of us have been pretty close now and you and him do business together. He should know by now I make smart decisions about all the shit I do, including women. I wouldn't have even recommended you as his property manager if I didn't trust you. Now all of a sudden he wanna ask if I'm making the right decision?" James's voice began to elevate.

"Babe, all I'm saying is——"

"He wanna fuck you MJ." James said to me seriously.

For a minute, I was at a loss for words but I quickly got myself together because this was the last thing I needed right now.

"Naw babe, see now you're tripping. You've just had a long day."

"Don't ever insult me like that again. I don't care how long of a day I've had. I'm always on point. And honestly, that's one thing I can say about you too when it comes to men. You can always tell when someone is trying to fuck you. Imma just fucking say it. You damn near make a living off of learning about men who wanna fuck you because that's how we've been closing these fucking deals. Don't lie to me MJ. Don't fucking lie to me! Did DC try to fuck you?"

I couldn't say anything. I didn't know what to say. DC not only tried to fuck me, but I let him. Shit! How was I going to get out of this mess? James totally caught me off guard with this conversation.

"Don't worry about it MJ. The look on your face says it all."

Gluttony

I can't believe Leo and I will be celebrating our twentieth wedding anniversary in a few weeks. I remember the day we met. I was in my junior year of college and interning for a fashion magazine because I wanted to be a designer. I thought that was going to be my foot in the door to my career so I would bust my ass trying to juggle school and my internship. I worked so hard because I just knew I would see my designs on the runway during New York Fashion Week.

Leo was working for a company delivering packages when he arrived at my internship with a box that needed to be signed by my boss. I thought Leo was so handsome. He kind of gave me Al B. Sure vibes because he was pretty fair skinned with curly hair and dreamy eyes. He was so polite when he asked me out unlike a lot of the fraternity guys I was dealing with at the time. Leo never attended college so I already knew my parents would have an issue with me dating someone like him. My parents were pretty bougie to say the least. They also despised my internship at the magazine but I fought them tooth and nail on it. They finally gave up trying to run my life and chalked it up to me just going through a "phase". I was a whiz at math so they felt I should at least try my hand at accounting but that was utterly boring to me.

When Leo and I got together, we were inseparable. We had dreams of having two kids, a dog, and a white picket fence. We got married literally a year after I graduated from college. I told Leo I wanted a house and that I wouldn't settle for anything else. We started learning about homeownership and because Leo adored me so much, he decided to work two jobs to ensure that we could purchase our first home together. All the while, I was attempting to run my own clothing line which was pretty much a flop. Leo was always so consistent when it came to working and saving income. He never made a ton of money but just enough to make sure we were okay. He let me figure out what I wanted to do with my life because designing clothes just wasn't proving to be lucrative for me.

I did have some interest in the homebuying process though when we started looking for a house. I told Leo I was interested in getting my real estate license and being the loving husband that he was, he not only helped me pay for my classes, he helped me study for the test as well. He was dedicated to seeing me happy. I ended up passing my real estate exam just a few months before I gave birth to our twin girls who are now sixteen years old.

Life was great. Anything I ever wanted, Leo always found a way to get it for me. When I found out I was pregnant with the girls, Leo decided to leave his previous job delivering packages and become a bus driver so that we would have decent insurance because he figured it might take a while for things to take off for me in real estate. He always thought ahead and even though he didn't have a college degree, he was very smart, strategic, and money conscious.

We've always had a pretty good life even when we didn't have a lot of money. But as time went on, I became more and more savvy as a realtor, and more driven by money. I'll never forget when I closed my first major deal, you couldn't tell me nothing. I bought a Mercedes Benz and splurged on purses, shoes, and jewelry. I literally blew through my whole check because I always knew in the back of my mind, Leo would take care of us.

I continued to soar in my career to the point I told Leo he really didn't have to work for the transportation company anymore and he could even pursue other endeavors now that my income could fund our entire lifestyle and more. He'd always wanted to become an engineer but because he couldn't afford to go to college, he just worked. And then of course when he met me and we had our girls, he sacrificed so much for us. I felt it was only right that he would have an opportunity to pursue his passion but now he feels he's too old to go back to school. He says he actually likes driving the bus but honestly, it has kind of cramped my style over the years.

Whenever I want to go away on a trip with him, I have to figure out if his driving schedule coincides with it. He drives public transportation, so he deals with a lot of crazy and ignorant people on a daily basis. I don't ever get to see him outside of his work uniform and that sucks because he's an amazing looking man. Somehow, he still finds time to workout because he really values his health. The one good thing I will say about his job is the health insurance. Seeing that he's been employed with the company for about fifteen years now, our benefits are superb.

Leo is really everything a woman could ask for. He's an amazing dad to our girls as he's the one who taught them how to ride a bike, drive, change a tire, defend themselves, how to deal with boys, and he's never missed a daddy/daughter dance. I mean, the list goes on. Tisha is the overachiever as she's a cheerleader, she's on the debate team, the national honor society, straight A student, and volunteers at a shelter. Tara on the other hand is a bit of a wild card who has skipped school pretty often, got caught smoking weed at twelve years old, also got caught sucking some boy's dick when she was fourteen years old, and was suspended a few times from school for fighting. I had to pull some serious strings to get Tara into Journey to Excellence with her sister because based on her profile, they weren't having it.

The only time I really saw Leo take a significant amount of time off work was about a year ago because he felt one of us needed to spend more time with Tara. He said that she was crying out for attention and sure enough she was. Leo and Tara bonded so much during that time and because of that, her behavior and grades significantly improved. She wasn't skipping school anymore and she even made the honor roll for the first time ever in her junior year of high school.

Eventually, Tara disclosed to Leo that she was gay and had been feeling that way for quite some time but wasn't sure if she was just liking one girl in particular or if she just liked girls in general. I mean, I guess there were things I noticed all along about Tara even when she was a little girl. She loved dressing up in Leo's clothes, she always wanted to try peeing standing up and would yell at me everytime I made her sit down, she loved sports and even tried wearing a jockstrap while playing football with Leo. She always commented on how "fine" women were that she saw on television, and I found lesbian porn on her phone a couple of times but just chalked it up to teen curiosity.

When she was caught behind the school sucking some boy's dick, I was heated but at the same time I thought maybe she wasn't gay after all. Later on, we found out it was just a dare because Tara is so competitive that she actually felt she could outsuck a boy's dick better than her friend. I tell you, the shit that teenagers think and do sometimes is beyond me. Tara also had the androgynous look down to a science. She would rock the whole "tomboy" vibe but she also loved wearing makeup, lashes, and getting her nails done so I couldn't always pinpoint which way she would eventually go with her sexuality.

Leo has been great with Tara though. He really listens to her and understands her. He allows her to be herself with no judgment. Tara thinks I don't understand her and that I favor Tisha over her. I mean, I guess there's some truth to that but hell, I didn't exactly sign up for this. I've never really had gay friends and there aren't any gay people in my family that I'm aware of. Unlike Leo, one of his favorite aunts is gay and has been openly gay since the '70s so I feel like he just has a better understanding of all of this.

Even with all of the great things I could say about Leo, I've been slowly losing interest in him in the past five years or so. He just doesn't excite me anymore. We're great friends and we get along so well. He treats me like a queen but there's absolutely no spark or chemistry. Sex is a total snoozefest. It's the same position all the time and even though I have orgasms during sex with him, they aren't really good ones. I just know how to get off because I know my body and what I need to do to get there, but there are no fireworks. We haven't really gone out on a date in forever, his jokes aren't really funny, he doesn't enjoy going out to events with me so when he's there, it's apparent he doesn't want to be, he tends to wear the scruffy look often and only shaves maybe once or twice a month, and honesty, he's just no fun. He's a good man though. He's solid and he would do anything for me and the girls but I've been craving so much more from him.

Our twentieth wedding anniversary was fastly approaching and I hired one of the best planners for our trip to Greece. Of course, I took it upon myself to even make this trip happen because if I didn't, we'd be left with Leo's plans to go to Miami yet again for another anniversary. At this point, I'm just planning an elaborate anniversary to save face.

I started sleeping with Damon who's a prominent politician in Chicago about six months ago. We met at a gala last year and immediately when we talked, I felt an electric current run through my body I hadn't felt in years. The power, prestige, and downright swag he exuded literally made me want to risk it all on sight. When I introduced myself to him, he stated he was already familiar with me due to my kick ass reputation as one of the top commercial realtors in the Midwest.

I loved how professional he could be, but with a bit of a dirty mouth. I yearned to get to know him more. He asked if we could exchange numbers to discuss a business opportunity, but by the way he looked at me, I knew that was code for he would like to mix business and pleasure and I was all here for it. I'd never cheated on Leo as in, I hadn't had sex with anyone else while we were married. Of course, friendly banter and slight flirting in between business deals would take place sometimes between colleagues, but nothing further. With Damon, he just felt like everything I was missing. He was extremely charming, very easy on the eyes, a gentleman, and he carried himself with so much confidence. He talked to me as if I was the only person in the room who mattered to him. I couldn't get enough of it.

I remember the first night we had sex. He asked me out to dinner and when I arrived, I didn't realize he orchestrated to have the entire restaurant closed to the public so that it would be a private event for two. He was good friends with the head chef who cooked one of his premiere dishes just for us. After that, the tigress in me came out and we fucked right there in the restaurant! The way he licked my pussy was just how I liked it too. He started kissing the lips while my thong was still on so it was the slow build for me. I loved how he teased me to the point I was yearning for more. He slid my thong over and let his tongue massage my clit. When he slowly took my panties off, he spread my legs wide and he began to perform a series of tongue gymnastics on my pussy that probably made me look like I was having a seizure. When he came up to kiss me, I could smell my sweet scent all over his beard.

It felt like a scene out of a movie as he pinned me up against the window overlooking downtown Chicago and held my waist from behind while going deeper and deeper. If anyone had a telescope to see on the twenty-fifth floor, they would've caught every bit of my double d's sliding up and down that window. I felt so free, so alive, and so sexy.

It's like Damon's dick was made just for me. The length, the width, and the girth was everything I could've wanted and more. Right then, I knew I would be completely sprung for this man. After I'd experienced several climaxes that night, he asked if I was ready to receive him. I told him yes but under one condition—he had to squirt all over my face and chest. His eyes bulged with excitement and so did his dick. I'd been wanting to express my kinky side to Leo for so long but he was so content with the most vanilla sex ever. This part of me had been bottled up for years and I felt like I was going to explode. Well, I got the opportunity to live out my fantasy with Damon as he obliged my request. I wanted to be engulfed in every part of him and I enjoyed all of it. I seriously had no remorse because I felt I had been deprived sexually for so long, I'd convinced myself that I deserved it.

Every sexual encounter with Damon after that just got better and even riskier. We fucked in the elevator of his office building during the middle of the day, we fucked in a community center he was speaking at for a fundraiser, we fucked in one of the conference rooms at a convention center while meetings were in session, we fucked in one of the commercial real estate properties I was showing him, hell, we even fucked in a church for which he was a guest speaker that day. The stakes just got higher and higher and I became so addicted to the rush.

I was a bit reckless one time as Leo stumbled across some messages between Damon and I on my iPad that I stupidly left on our bed because I was in a rush to a Journey to Excellence meeting for the girls. I couldn't even play it off if I wanted to because it was very clear that Damon and I were planning to meet up and have sex. I even sent Damon some nudes to go along with the invitation. The crazy part is, I didn't even feel bad after months of sleeping with Damon. I just felt bad that I'd gotten caught.

Leo was extremely upset with me but he never once called me out of my name or even tried to kick me out of our home. He actually suggested marriage counseling because he said he could tell something was going on and that I'd seemed kind of distant but he didn't have proof of me cheating. He said he was willing to work through it if I was. I was so shocked because I think I secretly wanted Leo to just ask for a divorce so that I could be with Damon, but again, that's not Leo. He truly believes in the sacredness and sanctity of marriage. He said that he signed up to love me for better and for worse and he said infidelity was the worst for him but he wasn't willing to throw in the towel. Leo said in order to move forward, I would have to cut all ties with Damon and instead of owning up to what I really wanted, I told Leo I would commit to that.

I'd tried everything to "bring the spark back" including going to weekly counseling sessions where I basically would sit there and lie to Leo and the therapist each week to make it seem like I'm giving my full effort. I even continuously endured the most basic ass sex ever to appease Leo. All the while, Damon was consistently rocking my world. I kept trying to figure out how to keep my affair from Leo but also not trying to be the bad guy in this situation. It wasn't exactly a good look for us to divorce within the circles we were intertwined in and that's by my own doing because Leo really isn't into the whole elite world. He just does it to satisfy me.

The last time Leo and I were watching tv, he accidentally sat on the remote and the channel changed to one of the news stations. Damon was being interviewed about a nonprofit organization that he wanted his constituents to invest in. I didn't realize the channel had changed because I was in the kitchen grabbing another drink when I heard a loud sound. I ran into the living room to see if Leo was okay, but he'd gotten so upset with seeing Damon's face on the screen that he threw the remote and knocked over one of our vases.

"I can't believe how this motherfucker parades around for the people all the while he was screwing my wife!" Leo yelled and was breathing rather hard.

I didn't know what to say as we had been in counseling for well over three months at this point and even though I was secretly still fucking Damon, I thought Leo was moving past my infidelity.

"Uum, Leo what the hell? You just broke one of my favorite vases!"

"I don't give a fuck about that vase. Why is he still in office?" Leo pointed to the tv.

"I don't want to upset you more than you already are, but why would he not be in office?" I asked nervously.

"If he could fuck another man's wife so casually without any remorse, who's to say what other underhanded shit he's doing? I heard from another bus driver who said he's been stealing money from organizations he so-called supports."

"Babe, we don't know that."

"Don't you fucking defend him."

I thought the most upset I'd seen Leo was when he initially found out about Damon and I, but this was on another level. I'm not sure if this was the residual effects of me cheating or something else. He'd never even shown this level of anger in counseling. I just couldn't understand what triggered him.

"I wasn't trying to defend him. I apologize if it seemed that way. I've just never seen this side of you before and we've known each other forever." I tried to sound calm.

"I've been working really hard to get past what you did. I honestly do forgive you. But I keep telling myself I better not come across that dude on the street or I'm fucking him up on site."

I just stood still because it seemed like anything I could say at this point might set him off. I thought about what our counselor said about me not dismissing Leo and validating his feelings if he brings up the affair.

"I'm so sorry I've caused you this much pain. You have every right to feel the way that you feel."

"Leilani, I believe we should expose him. He doesn't deserve to be mayor, let alone in any office for that matter."

Leo rarely ever calls me by my first name. I've always been Lee Baby or LeLe to him so I know he's livid. Again, I really didn't know what to say.

"If it's okay to ask, what do you mean by expose him?"

"Just like I said, expose. Don't you know the definition Ms. College Graduate?"

Oh shit, Leo was really hurt and trying to stick it to me at the same damn time? I knew that Leo had never been jealous of me getting my degree, especially because I offered to take care of things financially so that he could go back to school, but *he* said he didn't want to waste his time going to college.

"Okay, maybe I should paraphrase the question. How do you think we could expose him?" I asked calmly even though Leo could really kiss my ass at this point with that last comment he made.

"I don't know! You're the one with all the connections. I'm pretty sure you can provide an anonymous tip to someone so that the information could start circulating." Leo said angrily.

Leo walked out of our front door and slammed it. I looked out of the window and noticed him walking down the street. Leo was definitely the kind of man to leave the house for a while and take a walk when something was weighing heavily on his mind. It used to bother me during the earlier years of our marriage because I felt like he should've always told me where he was going but then I just got used to it. He always came back home in a few hours and it wasn't like he ever returned verbally or physically aggressive towards me. That's just how he dealt with his frustrations. I hated that Leo was so upset but I was still so drawn to Damon. I couldn't get him out of my system and I damn sure wasn't going to help Leo expose Damon because then that would expose us! I really don't think Leo is even thinking straight right now. None of this made any sense.

I debated whether or not to tell Damon about what Leo wanted to do. Part of me didn't want to get into any of this right now with him, but I would be lying to myself if I denied the fact that I wanted to hear his voice.

My conversations with Damon had been a bit limited since Leo found out about my affair so I had to up the ante a bit on my sneaking around. I actually ended up getting a separate phone so that Damon could text me a bit more freely. I'm just too grown for this shit. I really want to be with Damon. I just feel like I've really outgrown Leo and honestly, no amount of counseling is going to help that. I decided to call Damon anyway. I was in the house by myself and the girls were spending the night at my mom's house.

"Hey sexy, I miss you so much." I said in my school girl tone. I always got a bit giddy around Damon as he brought that out of me. I looked up to him so much. I felt like I was always learning something from him.

"Hey hun, what's up? It's definitely good to hear from you. I'm actually surprised that you called."

"I know I've been a bit incognito. You know my situation right now."

"Of course, but is this what you want, Leilani? I could give you everything and so much more."

"I know you can and I want you too. It's just not the easiest thing to leave a marriage of almost twenty years with two teenagers. I have a reputation too, you know?"

"Trust me, I understand your position. The spotlight has been on me heavily my whole career. At least when I got divorced years ago, I was still grassroots and no one even knew who the hell I was so I get it."

"Damon, I really need to talk to you about something." I sighed.

"Okay? This sounds a bit serious."

"Leo saw you earlier on the news and he flipped. He broke my vase and——"

"Wait, what? Did he hit you?" Damon's voice elevated.

"No, no. It's nothing like that. He just got really upset and threw the remote and it hit my favorite vase. I was in the kitchen at the time. I'm fine but——"

"What is it Leilani? I've never interfered in your life at home. I know my place but I'm not liking the direction this is going."

"Leo could've just been really upset when he said this but he said he wanted to expose you."

"Expose me? For what? Oh, because he can't satisfy his wife he wants to act like a simp?"

"Okay, let's calm down for a minute. I doubt he does anything. He doesn't have the power or means to."

"Again, like I asked, what is he trying to expose me for? Having an affair with a married woman? Trust me, my public relations team would be all over that." Damon said confidently.

"Not just the affair Damon. He mentioned some crazy talk about a bus driver friend of his said you were stealing some money from some organizations. Like seriously, what does he know?" I chuckled.

It was quiet on the phone for a minute. I didn't know if it was a bad signal or if the silence meant something else.

"Damon!" I yelled.

"I'm here Leilani."

"Sorry I yelled like that. I thought I lost you there for a minute."

"Who is this bus driver that he's talking about?"

"His friend is named Rick Barfield. They started working for the transportation company at the same time. I'm pretty sure it's just Rick being Rick always talking about how dirty politicians are without really knowing anything"

"Did you say Barfield?"

"Uum, yeah? What's the problem?"

"By any chance is Rick related to Eric Barfield?"

"Yeah, he has a brother named Eric. Why?"

"Shit! Eric and I have always been enemies. Eric was the president and CEO of the Chamber or Commerce in our hometown before I ran for mayor. I can't lie, I found out some information about him and I blackmailed him for it in the past. He eventually resigned from the Chamber because of that. He said he would eventually get me back in the worst way. Fuck!"

"How is that possible if it's not true?"

"Here's the deal. It's a long story and it's going to be hard to explain all of this over the phone."

"No, it sounds pretty cut and dry to me because it's either true or it isn't."

"It is, but I can explain."

I couldn't believe I'd gotten myself wrapped up in this mess. What was I going to do now? I'm practically in love with this man and this is how this shit goes down? I felt like such an idiot.

"Look Leilani, it's not what you think. I'm not that man anymore. When I was running for office, yes, I made some deals with some folks that involved some large sums of money. I wanted to win. It helped my campaign significantly but you know I'm for the people. I never hurt anyone but I didn't have a fighting chance against my opponent because I didn't have the money. The people loved me but I didn't have the influence of money and power on my side so I took a different route. In order to play this game, you can't play by the rules. I know it's dirty but that's politics baby."

"So what else are you lying about? I'm pretty sure there's more. Why would you stop at just this? I felt my blood boiling at this point.

"I know you're upset but all I can say is, Leo cannot pursue this and I need you to stop him. This could cost me my entire career! And what about us?"

"What the fuck you mean what about us? There is no more us Damon."

"Leilani, look at my world. I could give you everything. You can travel anywhere as much as you like, and experience anything you like."

"I have my own money, Damon. I'm pretty legit too, you know?"

"Oh, I know, but think about us together. We could be a force. As much as you try to deny it, I know you like the spotlight, the private jets, the islands to ourselves, a bank account triple the size of what you have now, and let's not forget the sex. I know you want to experience that on a regular. We both be feigning for each other, but Leo cannot blow this shit up. If he does, your name will come out too and everything you've worked for could go down the drain. We can't let this happen."

I just couldn't believe this. What was I going to do? As angry as I was with Damon, I believed he was being truthful with me about the money and everything else he said. I honestly didn't feel like he was a conniving person at all. I saw so much good in him and the way he cared for me is what I'd been craving for so long, but what the hell was I going to do about Leo? I had a funny feeling he was not going to let this go. He was determined to make sure Damon paid for having sex with me and he really thought if he was exposed for embezzlement, that would give him the satisfaction.

"I can't believe I'm saying this Damon, but the only way Leo won't be able to expose you or us for that matter is if he were dead."

As soon as the words came out of my mouth, I knew I couldn't take them back. I've known for a long time I wanted to be with Damon but I didn't have the guts to divorce Leo and I knew for certain he wasn't going to divorce me. My only way out was if Leo was no longer alive. That would be the only way I could save face and also keep Damon from being exposed. Shit, Damon is going to think I'm some crazy bitch to even think of wanting my husband dead.

"Well, it looks like we know what we have to do." Damon's voice sounded distant but certain.

"Please don't think I'm an evil person for even contemplating this. I've never in my life even killed a fly. It's not like me to wish death on anyone." My voice trembled.

"Trust me, I know you don't have an evil bone in your body, that's why I'm going to take care of everything. So from here on out, I don't want you saying anything else about this because I don't want you attached to any of this. The less you know the better so that you have no connection to what is about to happen."

"I'm sick to my stomach thinking about this. What about the girls? What about my in-laws, and his friends? I can't believe this is going to happen?" I began crying on the phone.

"Babe, I know this hurts but this is the only way we can keep from tarnishing our reputations and so that we can be together. Unfortunately, Leo is a liability so he has to go. It's our only way out."

"Oh my God Damon! I hear Leo's keys in the door. I've got to go!" I tried to hurry off the phone.

"Okay, no worries. We'll talk soon, but like I said, I'll handle it."

Damon hung up the phone and I rushed upstairs and locked myself in the bathroom to get myself together before Leo saw my face. He would easily be able to tell I'd been crying and would drill me about what was wrong until he got an answer. Why did I tell Damon that Leo needed to be dead in order for this scandal to not come out? I couldn't think of anything else?

Like, seriously? Have I wanted my husband dead all along? What kind of person was I?

"Leilani, where are you?" Leo yelled from downstairs.

"I'm coming! I'm in the bathroom." I yelled back.

I touched up my makeup, especially my concealer to hide a little bit of the puffiness under my eyes from the tears. I ran back downstairs and tried to appear normal.

"I'm sorry I walked out like that LeLe. It just hurt to see his bitch ass on the screen. It just pains me to even think about that man having his hands on your body."

"I know, baby, and I'm sorry. I know no amount of words will change what happened." I attempted to console Leo by hugging him and rubbing his back at the same time.

"Babe, I really need you to do something for me." Leo said while intently looking me in the eyes. Last time he asked me to cut all ties with Damon. I imagined he just wanted to remind me to have no dealings with him ever again.

"We really need to expose him for the fake politician he is. If you want our marriage to work like you say you do, you'll go through your contacts of powerful people and make this happen. This is how we can move on for good. Once he's found out, he'll lose his position as mayor, and will probably have to pay a hefty fine. He just needs to go. Can you do that for me?"

Leo was really serious about this and I had absolutely no idea what to do. He was really forcing my hand. I just couldn't believe my only way out of this was to have Leo killed. I had to think fast otherwise, Leo would start questioning my motives.

"Uum, let me look and see who would even have the power to help this come out without us being tied to this. We have to be very strategic or we could go down as well." I was stalling at this point but I knew Leo would fall for it.

"Okay, you've got a point. Thank you for doing this babe. I've been trying to move on from all of this but seeing him on tv was just a reminder of everything that's happened. Thank you so much for understanding. I've never asked you to use your influence for anything but I need you for this right now."

"Okay babe, I understand. And again, I'm sorry." A tear fell from my eye but not due to remorse but because I knew what I had to do.

"It's okay LeLe, we're going to make it through this. We're not giving up on almost twenty years of marriage. We're in this together."

Leo kissed me on my forehead and hugged me. I tried so hard not to shake in his arms due to the fear I had inside me. All I could think about was this being the last time we'd probably hold each other like this again.

* * *

My heart was literally pounding so hard I thought it was going to leap out of my chest. I'd just arrived at a warehouse for a final walk through of a showing. I was sitting in my car with sweaty palms while looking around to see if anyone was watching me before I headed into the building. Damon and I had previously spoken about the plan regarding Leo this morning. I never thought in a million years that I'd be planning to have my husband murdered. I was in so deep at this point that I could barely see straight. Damon was handling all the specifics including hiring the hitman so that the execution would be clean, precise, and of course leaving no trace of our involvement.

I could not sleep at all last night because everything from the girls finding out that their dad was dead, to the news spreading like wildfire, and even down to the funeral services were playing out in my head. I often wondered how I would live with myself. I confided in Damon about my feelings of being scared and wondered about the aftermath once his plans to kill Leo went through. He mentioned that it would definitely be a tough road ahead for me due to my conscience but that we would get through it together. I often wondered how cold and calculating a person would have to be to pull this off, but Damon was always so compassionate and attentive to my needs that it almost seemed impossible that he would even come up with this plan.

Part of the plan was me asking Leo to meet me at the warehouse for a final walk through of the property because I wanted us to celebrate by going out to dinner afterwards. From there, we would leave the warehouse together but then I would state that I left something in the building while Leo walked to his car. A black SUV with tinted windows and no visible license plate would quickly roll past him and open fire leaving Leo for dead before I make it out of the building.

I was having so many second thoughts racing through my head. I just didn't feel like I could go through with this. I was experiencing shortness of breath to the point I felt like I was having a mild panic attack. I decided to call Damon before heading in.

"Hello?" Damon's voice sounded far away.

"I can't breathe. I thought I could do this but I can't. I just can't!" I said while gasping for air.

"Okay Leilani, I know you're scared. We've gone over this numerous times. There's so much at stake for both of us so if we don't do this, everything could backfire. Leo is not going to rest until my whole life is in shambles. We can't take that risk. And this isn't just about our careers. We came into each other's lives for a reason. We're supposed to be together. As long as Leo is alive, none of that will be possible. I know this has been a lot for you and I wouldn't dare minimize the years you all have had together and the life you've built, but remember, Leo is forcing our hand. We really have no choice at this point." Damon tried to convince me.

"But there's always a choice Damon. It may not be the one we want to make but we can't kill a person just because we're worried about the outcome of a situation. I just believe we can come up with another plan." I said desperately.

"Leilani, there is no other plan. We have to do this and we have to do this now."

Every word that Damon spoke sounded unclear. I could no longer make out what he was saying because I felt myself slipping into a bit of a fog. I felt like I couldn't even see straight. My hands felt extremely clammy and when I looked down, I imagined blood on my hands and I let out a loud scream.

"Leilani! What is it?" Damon yelled.

"Damon, I really can't do this. You have to call the hitman and stop this. I just can't do this." I urged.

"It doesn't work like that Leilani. Everything has been put into motion. We just can't stop it."

"I'm begging you! I see Leo's car pulling up. Please, I'm begging you!"

"Just trust me."

And then Damon hung up. All of a sudden, my car felt cold and then it started to rain outside. I felt the tears welling up in my eyes but I had to control it because I couldn't let Leo see me like this. I got out of my car and walked over to Leo's car to greet him.

"Hey babe, how long will this take? I'm actually really hungry." Leo chuckled.

Thoughts of Leo lying on the ground in cold blood popped up in my head and I felt like I was going to throw up.

"It won't be too long. Let's head in right now out of this rain and hopefully this will be quick so we can get something to eat."

"That sounds like a plan to me." Leo said while smiling at me. My heart felt like it had broken into a million pieces. He looked so innocent.

We walked into the building but my client hadn't arrived yet. I pretended to make a follow up call to the client so Leo wouldn't suspect anything. I headed into one of the offices in the building to call Damon but he didn't answer. I tried calling Damon back to back three times but he still didn't answer. I couldn't leave a detailed message because we couldn't leave any evidence of the plan. I attempted to leave a cryptic text message indicating I really wanted him to not go through with this but still no response. I seriously felt like I was going to pee on myself at this point because I was so nervous.

"Lele, no luck?"

Leo scared me as he popped up in the office behind me and I made a screeching noise.

"Whew, you scared me! But no luck. My client hasn't picked up." I nervously chuckled.

"Are you okay, you seem a bit on edge?" Leo asked in a concerned tone.

I noticed I was tapping my pen on the desk and I felt a wetness underneath my arms and in between my chest as I was starting to sweat profusely. Thankfully, I had on all black so it wasn't exactly noticeable.

"Uum, yeah I'm fine. I just know that you're hungry and my client is taking a long time."

I looked outside and noticed it began to grow a bit darker. This really felt like a scene out of a movie. I was so scared.

"Well, just try calling your client again. I'm going to take a look around while I wait for you."

Leo walked out of the office with an oblivious look on his face. He had absolutely no clue that this would be his fate and at the hands of me of all people! I had to stop this one way or another. Then my phone rang. It was Damon finally.

"Listen, don't say anything. You need to make sure that Leo is heading outside in the next five minutes. No earlier or later." Damon said.

"I know, but I can't do this. I just can't. I've really thought about this Damon. Leo loves me like crazy and I can't do this to him." I whispered as my eyes began to water.

"We don't have time for this. He has to go now!" Damon yelled.

I'd never heard him talk to me like that. I was afraid that now maybe Damon was capable of hurting me too. If Leo was going to go down, we were just going to have to go down together. I can't believe I even considered this in the first place. I figured if Leo and I went out the back door instead of the front and quickly walked across the street to the nearby building, the hitman wouldn't see Leo and just go away. I prayed that this worked but all I felt was a huge weight in the pit of my stomach. I knew I was such an amateur at this but I needed this to work.

I walked out of the office door straight towards Leo.

"We have to go now, but we need to go out the back door." I grabbed Leo's arm tight.

"What the hell——"

"Don't ask any questions Leo, I'm begging you. Just come on!" I screamed.

For the first time ever since I'd known Leo, I'd never seen him so concerned and speechless. He just said okay and we swiftly ran to the back door.

"As soon as I open this door, we need to run as fast as we can over to the building across the street."

"Lele, what is——"

"Please! I'm begging you! No questions! On the count of three... one, two, three!"

I busted open the door and as we ran, those few steps across the street felt like miles.. My heart was racing, I felt my ponytail coming undone, and I was holding onto Leo's hand for dear life. Right before we got to the door of the building across the street, I heard tires screeching and shots were fired.

"Leilani!"

I heard Leo scream extremely loud and I felt myself fall to the ground and everything went black. My eyes opened for what felt like only two seconds and I saw blood on my hands just like I imagined when I was in the car earlier. The first thing that came to my mind was that Leo was indeed shot. I kept hearing screams, but could no longer see anything. And then I heard Leo scream again.

"Leilani! Oh my God! Please someone help! My wife has been shot!"

Sloth

This is what I get for dating down. I should've stuck to my standards instead of giving men with "potential" a chance. When my girls Candice and Monica told me I was too hard on men and that I would end up being single for the rest of my life if I didn't loosen up a bit, I decided to give Tristian a chance. I mean it was kind of hard to resist him because he was fine as hell and I eventually found out he definitely knew how to eat the shit out of some pussy, but I should've known that wouldn't sustain a marriage.

Tristan and I locked eyes at a five star restaurant one day. I was dining with Candice and Monica while he was sitting at a table across from us with a few men for what appeared to be a business meeting. I was a bit intrigued as he was dressed in a well-tailored suit, with a fresh haircut, and shapely goatee. His complexion was a smooth caramel and he had dimples to match. I was pretty convinced that he was getting panties thrown at him left and right just by the way he looked. He appeared to be a bit younger too, like he was in his early to mid-thirties. I was already forty-five years old, never been married and with no children. He definitely caught my eye but I definitely wasn't checking for him initially. Candice and Monica noticed me and Tristian's eye contact and mentioned that I should say hi. I told them absolutely not as he probably still had his mother's breast milk on his breath. Monica mentioned age was nothing but a number and that I should shoot my shot. I had to remind her that I had a net worth of about five million dollars and I was not in the market to babysit a grown ass man.

Somehow, Tristan and I ran into each other after I excused myself to go to the bathroom. I honestly think he was following me so that it would look like we just happened to be in close proximity to one another when I started heading back to my table. He said he couldn't take his eyes off of me and that he was smitten by my beauty. He asked if I was married and I said no. He appeared excited by the look in his eyes and proceeded to initiate a coffee date. Even though I was used to first dates being a bit more extravagant, I went against my better judgment and I accepted his invitation.

Our initial date was amazing. We talked for hours on end and we learned so much about one another. He told me he was an appraiser and while I was happy to know that we were both in real estate, I wasn't exactly impressed with the fact that he probably only made around sixty to seventy thousand dollars a year if he was lucky but I kept hearing Monica and Candice in my head about trying to relax a bit. One thing that did impress me though was his physique. It was apparent that his bulging arms were a clear indication of dedication and hard work. I was definitely attracted to him, but I wasn't so quick to have sex with him because I really wanted to learn more about his intentions as it pertained to relationships.

He was quite assertive when it came to scheduling our first date, meeting me at the coffee shop and opening the door for me once he noticed I arrived, asking me what kind of coffee I liked but also offering suggestions of his favorite java and why, asking open ended questions to learn about me but also willing to share various aspects of himself, and paying and asking for a follow up date. Even though he was younger than me, I could tell he'd had practice in the dating world and appeared to know what he wanted. I actually liked the fact that he didn't throw around money on the first date to impress me so that I could get to know him. It was refreshing and a nice change for once. Maybe Candice and Monica were right and that I needed to be a little more flexible with my approach to dating.

After our initial date though, things were a bit rocky and inconsistent. Tristan started texting me instead of calling me which was a huge pet peeve of mine. I figured he probably had a girlfriend or baby mama stashed somewhere so I stopped answering his messages. He later told me he had a really busy month at work which was the reason he had less time to talk on the phone and answer calls. I started to just write him off but I kept thinking about the many successful men I was meeting who were jerks. I gravitated towards dating older men because they were much more established but I was growing extremely tired of the pretentiousness and arrogance that came along with dating men over 50. And I'll add that many of them were struggling to get it up anyway. Maybe a younger man was what I needed.

So I decided to try something new and date someone who was approximately ten years my junior and I truly found out what I was missing... multiple orgasms being one of those things; but we also had fun. We went to concerts, comedy shows, we ate out all the time and we traveled. Now of course, I paid for the higher ticket items like the trips and top tier restaurants but I really didn't mind because I liked spending time with Tristan. He made me feel quite young again and showed me how not to be so serious about everything. And like I said, the sex was the shit! His stamina was off the charts probably because he was a diligent gym rat and he was very disciplined when it came to his eating habits. He even inspired me to be a bit more health conscious as well.

We spent most of our free time together and so when Tristan decided to pop the question only six months after we started dating, I said yes with the quickness. Now even though I was a bit dick whipped, I wasn't dumb enough to not have a prenup. He was only bringing in about forty-five thousand dollars a year after taxes and I was worth way more than that. He did seem pretty ambitious though so I figured in a few short years, he could really work his way up the ladder and significantly increase his income. Boy, was I wrong.

One of Tristan's bad habits that I was completely unaware of was gambling. I didn't exactly see the signs at first. I knew he enjoyed the occasional poker nights with friends, but he never really talked about the specifics. He painted a picture as if he was just enjoying some male bonding time. Well, he lost about twenty-five thousand dollars one night due which was money I'd given him for an investment opportunity that he asked for my support with. I wanted to see him win specifically because a part of me knew he felt some kind of way about not being in the same tax bracket as myself, so I wanted to help fund his dreams.

As time went on, I started to witness lackluster efforts on his part as it pertained to building true wealth. He was so focused on getting rich quickly that he consistently would drop the ball with his financial decision making. He kept gambling even though he was smart enough to really make a name for himself in real estate, but he became lazy and he didn't want to put in the work anymore. The only thing he stayed committed to was the gym but outside of that, his work ethic really took a dive. He made so many excuses but when it came to hanging out with his friends, going to the gym, and going to so-called exclusive networking events which I still believe were just a bunch of parties for twenty and thirty something year olds, he was ready to go to that. It's as if he knew how responsible I was. He took advantage of the fact that not only would things be taken care of financially, money would be consistently pouring in on my end. I was pissed to say the least.

I tried talking to him about my concerns and told him I didn't have to put up with his laziness. This negro had the nerve to quote me some Kevin Samuels rhetoric about how hard it would be for me find a man because of my age and that I was too difficult to be in a relationship with. He said I was only focused on money and that I talked down to him most of the time which was totally not true. He was just inadequate and did not want to be held accountable. Little did he know, I had already moved on in my head and with my body.

We were in year three of our marriage and for the past two months, I was getting it on with a colleague of mine who was a building inspector. Adonis was engaged but we would fuck in the middle of the day on Wednesdays to be exact at five-star hotel not too far from my office.

I'd pretty much given up on men at this point. I felt like one big ole money pit with Tristan and I was only with Adonis because he knew how to hit my g-spot every single time along with making me squirt. I lived for those moments. Why couldn't I just find a man who did what the hell I said, spent tons of money on me, and fucked me like his life depended on it? Was that too much to ask?

I was so over Tristan and I hated coming home to him sitting on the couch making phone calls as if he was really doing real work. Today was one of those days but this time, some of his friends were over during the middle of the day. Like, what the hell?

"Tristan, can I talk to you for a minute?" I said as I dropped my keys on the kitchen counter signaling for Tristan to follow me in one of the guest bedrooms on the first floor so that we could have some privacy.

"Babe, that's kind of rude. You just walked in the house and didn't say anything to anyone." Tristan said in a low tone of voice while closing the bedroom door as if he was actually embarrassed by me.

"How dare you say I'm being rude? This is my house! What the fuck is going on? It's one o'clock in the afternoon. So don't none of your friends work?" I asked angrily.

"Trinity, conventional jobs are slowly becoming obsolete. David is an app developer, Greg is a YouTuber, and Journey is an influencer. We're building something together. I'm tired of the grind. Being an appraiser was not exactly what I planned for my life but hey, it paid the bills. I'm just not interested in making money that way anymore."

"Oh, so you've decided to live off of me while you figure out what you want to do? And why is another woman in my house without you consulting me first? That's hella disrespectful."

"Journey ain't thinking about me in that way, trust me. Her boyfriend is an NBA player and like I said we're working on building some things together. Journey has great connections and she knows about my background in personal training so she and Dave are helping me build an app to take my personal training business to the next level."

"Wait a minute! Since when do you have a personal training business?"

"I told you I wanted to use my personal training background and start my own business because I knew I could make more money in a day doing things this way as opposed to busting my ass as an appraiser and not having anything to show for it. Wow, you really don't give a damn about anything I'm trying to do, do you?"

"It's not that I don't give a damn, I just don't understand your methods for attaining wealth. It makes no sense to me."

"Like you said, it makes no sense to *you*. Everyone isn't trying to spend years acquiring the kind of money you have after years of working when I can do it in less time. It's just the way of the world now."

"This just isn't working for me Tristan. Yes, I knew you didn't have much money coming into this marriage but I was willing to work with you because you seemed dedicated and looking to work your way up. This just feels like a fad and get rich quick schemes. It takes more than that. It's the long game that leads to success. All this overnight success is a bunch of bullshit. Take Journey for instance. She's beautiful and appears to have had some work done on herself so she lucked up on dating an NBA player, but who's to say how long that will last? David appears to be Indian and we know how long their money is even without his app development company, and Greg looks to have created a YouTube channel at the right time as he probably spends his entire life on there. But you? You're black with no real wealth in your family history. I'm sorry but it's going to take a lot more than you think to make the kind of money you're envisioning."

"Wow, tell me how you really feel then Trinity."

"I'm just speaking facts. I shouldn't have to sugar coat this stuff for you. I've worked really hard to get where I am today and I'll be damned if I let you just live off of me. I knew I shouldn't have gotten married. This is clearly benefiting you more than me."

My hands were feeling cold as I noticed my air conditioning was up higher than normal. I wondered if one of his friends asked to turn the air conditioning up because I wasn't a fan of my house being this cold. It was actually making me more upset.

"You've got a lot of nerve saying this marriage has benefited me more than you. When was the last time you had a real relationship before me? Seriously though. Yeah, you have money but I'm the one that's showing you how to have fun, enjoy life, and let's not forget how I make you cum back to back."

"Please, I really don't need you for that either." I whispered under my breath.

"What the fuck did you say?" Tristan asked in a stern tone of voice.

The disgust on Tristan's face for a minute made me regret allowing that to come out of my mouth. I really didn't know what to say after that but I tried to get him to understand where I was coming from.

"All I'm saying is, I need to know we're in this together. It's hard for me as a working woman seeing you in this house tinkering around on a dream. I can totally help you get your realtor's license and we can build together."

"There you go again trying to change me. I don't want to be in real estate anymore. I'm not passionate about that. We have the money for me to put my energy and focus into personal training."

"Well, technically, *we* don't have anything." I said with an attitude.

"Man Trinity, that's a fucked up thing to say but seeing that you feel that way, go ahead and file for a divorce. I'm walking away with half anyway."

"You're not walking away with shit! I have a prenup, remember?"

"Trust me, you never let me forget. But that little comment you made earlier about not even needing me for sex? You set your own self up with that one because there's a little clause in that supposedly airtight prenup that entitles me to half of your fortune if I can prove you've been unfaithful in this marriage."

"I'll be damned if you take any of my hard earned money. You wish, but it ain't happening."

"Trinity you might be smart in the real estate world, but when it comes to relationships, you don't know shit."

"This is such a bitch ass move. If you would apply this much energy into working instead of trying to prove that I'm sleeping with someone else just so you can live off my hard earned money, you probably would be a lot further along. I don't have time for this. You'll be hearing from my attorney. In the meantime, get the fuck out of my house."

"You're funny. I ain't going nowhere. I'm about to go back out there and finish my meeting. Now in the meantime, *you* might want to think about your decision to get a divorce because I doubt you want to lose all of this."

Tristan appeared pretty confident as he walked away and had the nerve to slam my door. Did he really know something or was he bluffing? He turned into a complete jackass. I'm livid because I really thought having a prenup was going to protect me from all of this but clearly, it didn't. I refuse to go down without a fight. Never again will I trust another man. Never!

* * *

It's a shame when you find yourself still angry from the night before. I was anxious to get my back worked out by Adonis but it wasn't Wednesday. I called him anyway just to hear his voice.

"Hey baby, what's up?" Adonis said with his Arabic accent.

Adonis was tall, about six foot two, with smooth olive skin, jet black hair, and a big ass nose that made navigating my pussy so much fun. He was so classy in the way he walked, talked, and how he handled business. He was very meticulous about things, he had a strong work ethic and just overall awareness of himself. To be honest, he was really my type, but he was engaged and he and his fiancée lived together as well.

We hooked up one day after an inspection he was doing on a property. At the time, he wasn't involved with anyone but Tristan and had been married for over two years. Tristan had gotten on my nerves so bad and I was starting to feel depleted. Adonis could sense I was a bit uptight during an inspection as I was very short with him and he made a joke saying I probably needed some good sex to take the edge off. I looked him dead in his eyes and told him he needed to be the one to take care of that for me. Two hours later, we were having sex in his loft a few minutes away and we've been meeting up weekly ever since.

He met his fiancée a few months later which didn't bother me because I wasn't seeking an exclusive relationship with him, but I was pretty bummed when she moved in as I knew it would change the dynamics of what we had going on. Adonis assured me we would still have our time as he was adamant about booking a room weekly for our midday loving.

"I'm definitely in need of some play time with you but I know today isn't Wednesday." I sighed.

"What's wrong? You sound pretty stressed?"

"I am."

"Where are you?"

"I'm downtown right now." "Come swing by my place."

Whew, that was music to my ears.

"I'd love to but what about your fiancée?"

"She's out of town right now. But remember, I'd never suggest something if I thought it would put you in a precarious situation."

Adonis' sexy ass accent coupled with his grown man mentality, always did it for me.

"Okay, I'll be there in fifteen minutes."

"I look forward to seeing you. I hope you're wearing something sexy. Well, it doesn't really matter. I'm going to take it off of you anyway."

Adonis was so confident and sure of himself and he knew what I liked sexually. He's literally probably the only man I've ever been with who just knows what I like. I never have to teach or guide him and he does everything so willingly. Tristan stopped providing foreplay a long time ago and only focuses on fucking these days. That's another reason he turns me off because he doesn't warm me up anymore. He's become very selfish during sex and he thinks he's really pleasing me. Anyway, I was on my way to Adonis' to relieve some of this stress and get what I deserved, which is catering and attention.

I did a u-turn so quick to head over to Adonis' loft. It was such a beautiful late summer evening where the weather was still warm but not too hot and the sun was setting. The burgeoning colors of fall were a sight to see. I started playing some Maxwell in my car and just let the breeze tickle the scalp of my freshly installed goddess locs.

I allowed the thought of a much needed rendezvous to clear my mind from the argument Tristan and I had the other day. I pulled up to Adonis' loft and saw him waiting for me at the door with a soft smile. I got out of my car, whipped my hair, pulled down my dress as it rose up while driving, and quickly walked over to him and greeted him with a hug. We walked in his home together and as soon as he closed the door, I put my index finger to his mouth and watched him suck it while he looked me in my eyes.

"Hmm, you know what I like. The smell and taste of your pussy is always such a beautiful thing." Adonis said while sucking my finger.

I'd already ditched my panties in the car to put my finger inside me so that Adonis could taste it when I arrived. What I enjoyed the most about Adonis was his ability to be extremely sexual but he still had a very classy vibe about him.

His home had always been pretty immaculate even when his fiancée wasn't living there. He was tidy and orderly. He always kept a well stocked and versatile wet bar, earth tone colors warmed his home which made it so inviting, and his pride in his multicultural background was prevalent as it included african art on the wall and even a hijab on an accent table.

"I really need this right now." I said desperately while walking over to the couch to sit down.

"I can tell. Would you like a glass of wine and talk about things a bit more?

"You're so sweet, but I know we're just fuck buddies and I'm not trying to complicate things."

"Unless you're not trying to complicate things for *you*, I'm fine. I like you Trinity and I respect you. I don't have you in my home right now just for a good time. We can talk. As a matter of fact, I encourage it."

Adonis sat down next to me on the couch and began to run his fingers through my locs and then smiled at me.

"Your hair is really beautiful like this. But then again, you make anything look beautiful." "Don't talk to me like that." I said somberly.

"Okay, so you want me to be rough with you and talk to you like you ain't shit? C'mon now Trinity, that's not even in my nature." Adonis chuckled.

"I get that. It's just, I'm vulnerable right now and——"

"And I get it too. You came over to get a good fucking. I understand and I'll oblige."

Adonis smiled.

Adonis moved in closer to me and kissed my lips softly. It still felt a bit romantic but really, why would I expect anything less? At Adonis' core, he was so caring and attentive. Whatever he did, he did with intention. It's like he could tell I needed a bit more tlc than just being bent over so I allowed him to be himself.

Adonis rubbed his hand gently across my face and slowly moved down to my shoulder and then to the spaghetti strap of my dress and slipped one side of it off. Before I knew it, half of my dress was down leaving my right boob exposed. He began kissing and sucking my breast just right. He didn't pull on my nipple either. Thank God because I despised that. He gently sucked it causing my clit to engorge even more and my pussy wetter. He continued to suck on my titty and allowed his other hand to work its way in between my legs.

I effortlessly laid back on the couch and just enjoyed being pleased. My eyes closed, the moans began to come, and my body swayed to the motions of him fingering me. Then his face made its way down to my thighs. He pulled me by my hips and laid me flat on the couch so that I was comfortable. By this time, the inside of my thighs were extremely wet due to the abundance of my juices that were flowing. Adonis literally went into beast mode when he began eating my pussy. He started with softer strokes and gradually became more aggressive while licking my clit. He then used his nose to essentially pull my lips back, he grabbed my thighs and lifted them up, and that's when his tongue became a cyclone. I knew I wasn't going to be able to take it anymore and that's when I let out a huge squirt all over his face and couch.

"Oh my God! I was expecting to cum like that." I said while trying to wipe Adonis' face and couch until he assertively grabbed my wrist.

"Baby, I don't give a damn about this couch. I can have it cleaned." Adonis said while swiftly lifting me up and carrying me in his arms like a baby.

We were kissing while he was carrying me upstairs to his bedroom. He laid me down and stood at the foot of his bed. I could see how hard his dick was and when his pants and underwear dropped to the floor, my mouth literally started salivating and I crawled on all fours towards his dick and began sucking him, deep throating him, massaging his balls, and just getting sloppy with it. I wanted every bit of his dick in my mouth as I loved hearing him yearn for it. I could feel his dick pulsating in my mouth but he slowed down as I could tell he didn't want to cum just yet.

He placed his hands on my head and began slowly moving it back and forth, in and out, and I was willing to let him guide me wherever he needed me to go for optimal pleasure. My mouth was so full of his dick that I gagged a bit but I didn't stop because I was so turned on. My pussy was so wet that I felt like I was going to cum just off the sight of Adonis taking so much pleasure in my skills. Adonis' thrusts began to speed up while he was gripping my hair tighter. He was truly getting lost in ecstasy and it was making me wetter and wetter. I knew by the time I got on top of him, his dick would just slide right on in. I was that aroused and open for him. I couldn't wait to take in every inch of his big dick in my pussy.

All of a sudden we heard the door chime.

"Wait a minute, do you hear that?" I whispered nervously with Adonis' dick still in my mouth.

"Shit, I heard it too?" Adonis said while looking a bit disappointed that we stopped.

Adonis was standing still and I was motionless as well because it sounded like someone was coming into the house.

"You know what? I would've gotten alerted on my Apple Watch if someone was coming into the house.

"Okay." I said while trusting Adonis' words.

Adonis laid me down at the foot of the bed and opened my legs extremely wide. Clearly I was *really* in the mood because I wasn't typically that flexible.

"Damn Trinity, I just want to admire what you look like. Your pussy is so fucking beautiful and soft. Watching you drip like this is so sexy." Adonis said while holding my ankles.

"Well, come and get this because I need you inside me so bad."

As soon as Adonis' dick entered me, it filled me completely. Adonis was moving inside me as if he was slowly dancing to an R&B tune. I didn't want it to end because it just felt so good. This is what I call pleasure. The way he touches my body and finds so much enjoyment in pleasing me is what makes having sex with him feel like it's on a whole other level. He then turned me over, and entered my pussy from behind. He took a handful of my locs and grabbed them as he stroked me and slapped my ass.

"Fuuuucckkk. Your pussy feels so good." Adonis said as if he was about to lose control.

I quickly moved up so that his dick would come out of me and I began sucking his dick again. I wanted all of his cum to enter into my mouth and when it did, I sucked him even more until he couldn't take anymore.

"Damn, shit!" Adonis said while holding his head back, looking up, and gripping my head in his hands.

"I see that you liked that." I said after I swallowed.

"Did I like it? Shit, that was amazing."

Adonis and I laid in bed, while he spooned me and started running his fingers through my hair again.

"Wait! I think I heard the door chime again. Did you hear that?" I questioned.

"Yeah, I heard it again too."

Then we heard footsteps walking upstairs. I was paralyzed by fear. I couldn't even think of an escape plan because there was no way out of here except for the door or me jumping out of the window. It had to be his fiancée because who else could it be? Would she bust in and shoot our asses? I had absolutely no idea what this woman was capable of. The steps got closer and louder. It was clearly a woman because it sounded like heels clicking on the floor. And then the doorknob turned a bit and my heart started racing and pounding. Adonis looked at me with a spooked look in his eyes and mouthed to me not to move or make a sound. I couldn't even argue with him because I had no other choice but to follow his lead.

The knob turned a little bit more and then stopped. It was quiet for about five seconds which felt like an eternity. And then we heard the steps again and they became more faint as it sounded like whoever it was, was leaving. Adonis and I sat there for about one minute straight without saying a word until we heard the door chime and then gently close. It was like a scene out of a horror film.

"I'm going to see what's going on." Adonis whispered.

"Please do, just for peace of mind?" I said while shaking a bit.

"Yeah, sweetie, no problem." Adonis kissed my forehead and as I watched his bare chiseled ass walk out of the bedroom door, I just continued to admire the view. But then I quickly snapped back into reality. What if that was his fiancée? I started gathering my clothes and trying to see how I would leave without her seeing me. My heart started racing again just thinking about it.

"Fuck!" I heard Adonis say out loud in his hallway.

I popped up out of the bed quickly and ran out of the room towards Adonis.

"What's wrong?"

"I just saw my fiancée pull out of the driveway."

"So it *was* her that we heard. But why didn't she say anything?"

"Shit, I don't know. But this isn't good."

* * *

I can't believe this is happening to me. It had been a couple of months since Tristan and I had sex. We were barely speaking to one another and we were pretty much ships passing through the night at this point . This was by choice though. After our big argument about my prenup, Tristan really took that hard. We didn't check in on each other, we hung out at different times, we had different interests, and we only discussed business at this point. He was still doing appraisals but only because he needed to fund his lifestyle of partying and hanging out with wannabe influencer friends. He said he was still trying to start his personal training business but I still saw no evidence of it; but then again, we weren't really speaking to one another either.

I had been in communication with my attorney regarding the possibility of divorcing Tristan and what that would look like for me financially. My attorney did confirm that the clause indicated Tristan was entitled to half of my entire fortune if he could prove infidelity on my part which I thought was complete bullshit. So I decided to minimize my recent interactions with Adonis until I was able to get a handle on what was taking place on the homefront.

Adonis also told me he was trying to keep things pretty chill as well after his fiancée basically figured out he was fucking another woman. He said she never brought up the cheating incident but figured she was still aware of it and decided to accept it. He mentioned he was open with her at the beginning of their relationship about him loving beautiful and successful women and that sometimes he had a sweet tooth for one every once in a while. She said she understood as long as she didn't have to know about it. Adonis also comes from a wealthy family so I think his fiancée values that and doesn't want to lose that so she doesn't question him about his illicit affairs.

I decided to sleep in a little later which is something I rarely do but all I had on my schedule today was this inspection. Tristan was in charge of the appraisal and to say I was nervous about this was indeed an understatement. Seeing that we weren't talking much these days and Tristan tends to halfass his job, I didn't know what to expect. He said he'd hired a few family members in the business to complete the inspection but the way his family was set up, it wasn't looking too good. I really didn't want to ruffle too many feathers where Tristan was concerned because I didn't want him to get angry all over again and try digging up anything on me that he could use against me. This shit made me so angry because never in a million years would I have thought anyone would have the opportunity to take so much money from me that I worked so hard for.

I got out of my comfy upholstered king sized bed and stepped into my furry slippers to head to my master bathroom. When I walked in, I looked around to see my large windows that graced me with natural sunlight every morning, along with the large glass doors that encompassed a beautiful sauna, an enormous tub at the center point of my bathroom, a large walk in shower with floor inlays, premium light fixtures, surround sound to play my favorite tunes, along with a built in bench that could comfortably seat five adults. This was definitely my dream home that I purchased five years ago and I'll be damned if Tristan gets any of this in a divorce settlement.

I was a bit anxious though because my period was a couple of weeks late. I had been experiencing irregular periods lately and a bit of fatigue but my gynecologist just chalked it up to perimenopause symptoms but I knew something was different. I still bought a pregnancy test last night but I didn't want to take it until Tristan was out of the house.

I opened up the package as I felt my heart racing a bit. I peed on the stick first so that I could take a shower and not worry about the results until I was done. I pinned my locs up, turned on Apple Music playlist and allowed the soothing sounds of some chill hop music to relax me. When I stepped into my hot shower, I felt a sense of calmness rush over me until I started thinking about if I was indeed pregnant. Clearly, it wouldn't be Tristan's because we hadn't had sex in a couple of months so there was no way I could hide that from him. The only person I'd been intimate with was Adonis and I had to consider his relationship as well.

I'd never had any children, nor did I desire any until now. I experienced so much in life, made a ton of money, traveled the world, but never brought a life into this world. And to be honest, I wouldn't even be upset if Adonis didn't have a desire to be a father, but this would be my opportunity to leave my own personal legacy. I just couldn't imagine Tristan being able to take my money. There had to be a better way.

I let the hot water and soap suds from the shower gel run down my back and legs. I wished I could just freeze time right here. I didn't want to deal with the possible aftermath of my decisions but I had to face the music. I turned the water off, wrapped myself in a big, plush white towel, and stepped out of the shower. The walk over to my sink to look at the results of my pregnancy test was nerve-wracking. When I picked up the stick, I just stared at it and a tear fell from my eye. For the first time ever, I was going to be a mom. I couldn't believe it. It wasn't Tristan's, but at that moment, I didn't care. I was going to be someone's mother and I couldn't fathom giving that up.

* * *

When I arrived at the property that Tristan's cousins were in charge of inspecting, there was a huge ass orange sign on the door. I knew exactly what this was which made me lose my shit. I called Adonis right away and told him about it.

"Hey what's up? I haven't heard from you in a little bit. I miss you." Adonis' voice almost calmed me but I was too furious.

"You will not believe this shit! I should've known better to let his people handle this!" I yelled.

"What are you talking about?"

"There's a huge orange sign on the property that Tristan's cousins were hired to inspect.

Dammit!"

"I know."

"Why are you so calm about this?"

"I knew you would be upset for the both of us. I went ahead and stopped the work order once I suspected those guys were working without a permit. When I found out the city launched a recent investigation to see who was working without permits, I stopped that shit right away to avoid getting fined. When I checked out the property, everything was wrong including the overall structure support, the stair thread was about twenty three inches and you know it's supposed to be sixteen, the double bolt front and back porches weren't strong enough, they did single bolts instead, and the pipes were too loose. Trust me, there's more but I can tell by your silence that this is really upsetting you."

"Damn right I'm upset and it's embarrassing as hell. I don't know why I trusted him and let's not even get into the fact that he could possibly have access to half of my money!"

"Okay, calm down Trinity. We talked about this. He doesn't have any way of knowing and we've been keeping our distance for a while too. You're just stressed out."

"Like hell I'm stressed out. I'm fucking pregnant!" I blurted out before I had a chance to figure out how I was going to tell Adonis.

"What did you say?"

I hung up on Adonis because I needed time to figure out how I was going to deal with this. I decided not to answer Adonis if he tried calling back. I was just planning on lying to him later and saying my phone ran out of battery life until I had an opportunity to collect my thoughts and have that conversation with him. Adonis started blowing up my phone but I didn't answer. I just couldn't talk to him right now but I knew who I needed to talk to...Tristan. I quickly got back into my car and sped off.

"Hey Siri, call Tristan." He was no longer babe in my phone, just Tristan.

"Hello?" Tristan answered the phone but I could clearly hear noise in the background as if he was out.

"Where are you?" I asked in a demanding tone.

"I'm at the store up the street from the house. What's up?" Tristan asked as if he was entirely clueless of the crappy inspection job his cousins did.

"Can you be home in the next ten to fifteen minutes? We really need to talk."

"Okay? You good?"

"We'll talk about it when I get home." I ended the call and quickly sped home which took me about twenty minutes on the expressway.

I hopped out of my car and power walked to the door as I was still in my heels. I was actually holding my stomach as if my mind was already practicing what it was like to have a growing baby inside of me.

When I walked inside, of course Tristan was sitting on the couch like he didn't have a care in the world.

"Did you know that your cousins dropped the fucking ball on this latest inspection?" I said while removing my shoes at the front door. I couldn't see how women wore heels during an entire pregnancy. My feet were already hurting.

"What are you talking about? You're always complaining about something and half the time, I don't know what you're talking about. Just say what you have to say." Tristan said while opening up a bag of chips after I told him I despised food in my living room. I swear at this point, he was just doing stuff to irritate me.

"So your little cousins, Robert and what's his face uum, Tony did a fucked up job on the property over on Prairie. I'm too pissed to even go into detail but just know that the work order has been stopped because there's a shit load of stuff wrong over there and it was suspected that your cousins were over there working without a permit." I felt my voice elevating at this point.

"How did anyone know they didn't have a permit?"

"So you're confirming they were working without a permit? Great! This is just fucking great!" I screamed.

"Trinity, you really need to calm your ass down and quit talking to me like I'm a little bitch."

"I can talk to you any way that I want to talk to you and if someone else tells me to calm down one more time, I'm going to fucking scream."

"What the fuck is wrong with you? Okay damn, the inspection fell through. At least the work order was stopped and we didn't get fined."

"Are you serious right now? Did you say at least *we* didn't get found out? See this is the shit I'm talking about. Your nonchalant attitude about this is beyond me. You're really fucking things up. I can't take this shit anymore."

"Here you go again Trinity being overdramatic. Go ahead and say it again. You want a divorce right? That seems to be what you go to anytime you get upset now."

"You caused all of this and you're talking to me as if this is my fault. I'm sick of this and I'm sick of you!"

After I yelled, I attempted to make a dramatic exit towards the stairs to head to my bedroom but I got a little dizzy. Before I knew it, my knees buckled and I fell face forward onto the floor. Tristan rushed over to me but he couldn't catch me in time.

"Trinity!" Tristan yelled and turned me over so that I was lying on my back.

"Oh my God! I hope nothing happened to my baby." I was holding my stomach and tears were falling from my eyes.

"What did you say?" Tristan's face turned from concern to anger.

I just stared at Tristan knowing there was no way for me to wiggle out of this one.

Thankfully, the only thing hurting was my wrist when I broke my fall. All of a sudden, Tristan's facial expression morphed into a devilish smirk and that's when I could tell he knew he finally figured out how he was going to get half of my money.

Wrath

For as long as I could remember, I've always wanted to be an actress. I would dress up in wigs and fancy clothes and perform skits in front of my family during gatherings as early as five years old. It gave me a chance to escape reality and become another person because typically, I was an introvert. I definitely wasn't the loud or boastful type. I'd even been called meek and reserved. Whenever I would "get into character" so to speak, my confidence would skyrocket and I felt like I could do anything.

While in high school, I shined in the theater club and performed in plays and musicals. I'd gotten my first real acting gig when I was cast in the pilot of a sitcom. I was so excited because I was only sixteen years old at the time and I thought my acting career was about to take off but unfortunately, the show was canceled before it even aired. The cast were told it was due to budget cuts but I heard through the grapevine that the networks were trying to do away with positive images of black families on television.

I never gave up on acting though but I had to pivot because my stepdad passed away unexpectedly after the pilot fell through which left my mom having to figure out what we were going to do financially. I was the oldest of three so she looked to me to help out with the bills. She couldn't afford to send me to college, nor did I want to go because I wanted to be a full time actress. After we lost our home because we couldn't keep up with the mortgage payments, real estate started to pique my interest. I wanted to help my mom purchase a home again so in my quest to figure out how to do that, I discovered that I enjoyed learning about real estate and decided to pursue getting licensed as a real estate agent seeing that college wasn't an option for me at the time.

Real estate became a lucrative career for me in a short amount of time. By the time I was in my mid twenties, I was able to purchase my first home and my mom moved in with me. My brothers were also able to attend college which was something I was never able to do. I never lost sight of acting as I would still take sporadic classes and perform in a few local shows but I couldn't put as much time and energy into it as I would've liked because I needed to pay the bills.

One day my agent informed me of a teen drama she scored me an audition for that I was really excited about. Even though I was in my late twenties at the time, I was able to pass for a nineteen year old on screen due to my youthful face. I ended up getting the part and I took a six month hiatus from work to film. It turned out to be a good show but not good enough to be renewed for another season so there I was back on the grind of real estate.

Currently, I'm so ready to quit my job. Even though I initially found interest in it, acting is my first love and what I've always wanted to do. Real estate really has been a means to an end and thankfully, it's helped me invest in my acting career, but it's time to move on. I've gained much notoriety as an actress and for some reason, I just feel like my big break is coming soon.

My agent says that I have all the makings of a Hollywood actress because not only do I have the talent, but I have the "look". Everytime I audition for a part, the casting directors always say I resemble a shorter Naomi Campbell due to my slender frame, smooth chocolate skin, long hair, and just overall exotic look. I didn't always grow up feeling good about myself though, but acting really helped me with my confidence overall. When you're always on a stage being told to project your voice, dive into various emotions, memorize lines in a matter of hours, and continuously perform even when you make a mistake, it produces a high level of grit. I learned to really deal with the "nos" in this business which produced so much tenacity in me even though I'm typically pretty laid back. I'm something like a quiet storm. I may appear timid, but there's more that lies beneath the surface.

I didn't get much attention from boys in high school, but once I graduated and started filling out a bit more, I was sort of bringing all the boys to the yard. I crack up whenever I think about myself in that way because it's definitely not in my character tp brag. Meeting so many men on various sets really showed me how they operate. The games they play and the lies they tell to every other woman in the industry will get you caught up if you're not grounded but when I met my husband Hunter at a casting party, I was definitely drawn to him.

Hunter looked like someone I was supposed to know. He didn't draw much attention to himself through his voice but definitely through his aura and how he demanded attention whenever he stepped foot in the room. I thought he was a casting director when I first laid eyes on him because everyone flocked to him like a swarm of bees to honey. I'd never seen him before but he was absolutely beautiful. He stood about five foot nine or ten inches so he wasn't exactly tall, but you wouldn't know it because his energy seemed to make him tower over everyone. His Italian features were extremely prevalent; olive skin, green/hazel eyes, black curly hair, a bit of a pointed nose, and a strong jawline. He looked so serious all the time but he was extremely breathtaking to me. I wanted to get to know him professionally, but I also wouldn't have minded knowing him on a personal level as well.

I mustered up the courage to walk over to him and introduce myself.

"Excuse me. Hi, I'm Rose Marie. Are you the new casting director? It's a pleasure to meet——"

Before I could finish my sentence, everyone started laughing and I felt like I was left out of an inside joke all of a sudden. I immediately felt my confidence take a bit of a dive but while everyone was laughing, Hunter was staring intensely in my eyes as if he could care less what everyone was laughing at.

"Rose Marie! Girl, that's Hunter. He's not the casting director." One of the other cast members chuckled. She was also dressed very scantily clad with her breasts all in his face but he didn't pay her any mind, he was still looking at me.

"Oh wow, I'm so embarrassed." I said.

"You don't have to be. I'm not an actor. I just know plenty of people in the industry. I'm Hunter by the way." His accent made me swoon.

When Hunter smiled, I just wanted to reach out and grab him. It was as if the curtain unveiled the most beautiful smile underneath all that seriousness.

"Uum, so what do you do?" I stuttered.

"I'm a serial entrepreneur. I own the largest title company in the city and I own various clubs around the U.S." Hunter was flexing a bit but I was still enamored.

"Title company? Oh my goodness, please forgive me. You're Hunter Rossi? I'm so embarrassed. I'm a real estate agent by day. I've heard of you obviously in my line of work but I'd never seen your face. Wow, it's so nice to meet you." I blushed.

"Likewise beautiful. Hey, why don't we skip the rest of this party and I can take you out to a more appropriate place suited for someone like you?"

I was a bit taken aback by how forward Hunter was and what his intentions were but I was so curious to find out more about him.

"Okay? What did you have in mind?" I asked nervously but very intrigued.

"Trust me, very exclusive fine dining. I have a car waiting downstairs. We can ride together." Hunter said while pulling a cigar out of the lining of his suit jacket.

"Why don't I meet you there?"

"Stranger danger huh?" Hunter chuckled.

"It's okay babe, I don't bite, but I understand your hesitation. Let me have your number and I'll text you the address."

Hunter's take charge but sort of aloof demeanor wasn't exactly what I typically sought out in a man but I was so digging it.

I gave him my number and the rest is history as they say. He was definitely charming, assertive and confident, but I later on found out after seven years of marriage, he was also a serial cheater.

* * *

When I woke up to my cast mate sucking my titties, I knew I was in a world of trouble. I was angry and frustrated with Hunter for consistently cheating on me and being so jealous of my acting career. I was also ready to quit real estate altogether but a small part of me was still a bit nervous to take the full plunge because I often wondered if acting would only take me so far.

Even though I was still getting work and people were noticing me more for the shows and plays I'd been featured in, I still hadn't gotten my big break.

Donna was a fellow actress that I'd spent much time with on set the past three months. She was a veteran in the business and she really helped sharpen my skills. She was also an amazing listener and I'd found myself venting to her more often than I probably should have about my personal life. For people who aren't a part of this world, they often don't understand what it takes to succeed in this business but Donna absolutely did. She even tried to offer advice as far as Hunter was concerned, but she really didn't have much sympathy for him because he was constantly cheating on me. Donna was also a very proud polyamorous lesbian who didn't exactly believe in the institution of marriage so she always told me that life was too short to not be fully enjoying what I wanted to do. What she didn't realize was, I actually enjoyed being married and monogamous but clearly Hunter had his own agenda.

"Donna, what are you doing? I can't do this with you." I said while pulling down my shirt and gathering my things still trying to figure out how I ended up in her bed.

"Do you remember anything about last night? After a long rehearsal, the cast decided to go out and you finally let your hair down for once and enjoyed yourself. You had a bit too much to drink so I offered to drive you back to my place. You did get a little frisky with me but I didn't take advantage because you were wasted of course. I even slept on the couch so you wouldn't think I was on some sneaky shit. But, when I came into my room this morning to check in on you, you asked me to lie down with you and hold you so hell, I did. You were telling me how much you appreciated me and then you kissed me. And shit, you're sexy so I kissed you back. I can't help that my lips made its way down to your titties."

"But you know I'm married! And you know I'm not a lesbian!"

"Oh stop. The chemistry has been strong between the two of us for a minute now. I understand you not wanting to admit that to yourself because you're married to a man and everything, but you can't deny what's between us."

Donna was what you would classify as butch. She wore a buzz cut and was physically fit with very toned arms and legs. The combination of masculine and feminine energy she exuded was quite enticing. She was white but something about her outlook on life and vernacular at times seemed as if she grew up in the hood. She was wearing a fitted tank top and basketball shorts and a locket necklace. The picture inside was of her deceased brother who committed suicide. She was such an advocate of mental health which is why she always pushed for me to live my life and my truth. But just because I was attracted to her didn't mean I was gay. She just paid attention to me, listened to me, and she happened to be attractive.

"There isn't anything between us. It was a mistake. I was drunk and I have a lot going on."

I started to scan Donna's room and noticed the literature on her shelf about ethical non-monogamy and Black Lives Matter. There was also a rainbow flag and tapestries on her wall, crystals and plants on her window sill, and of course, a strap-on propped up on her nightstand. I definitely could tell Donna probably got a lot of action off of her vibe alone.

"Listen, I'm not here to force you to do anything and I'm definitely not trying to entertain anyone that's bi-curious. I was just letting the moment do its thing. I saw you staring at my night stand though." Donna winked at me.

"Uugh, stop. I really need to get home. Thank God Hunter is out of town. Otherwise, this would be such a mess right now."

"Fuck Hunter. He's such a douche. He's probably bending some bitch over right now and you're sitting over here feeling sorry for yourself and shit." Donna lit up a blunt while sitting on the edge of her bed.

"You know what? I'm not going to sit here and listen to this. Where are my pants?"

I was looking under the covers and under the bed trying to figure out where the rest of my clothes were.

"Just relax. Let me at least make you some breakfast before you head out and start calling him incessantly."

"You think you know me so well." I said while still trying to find the bottom half of my wardrobe.

"Well, I think I kind of do with everything you've shared with me."

Donna touched my hand and when she looked at me, she leaned in and kissed me softly and for a minute, I allowed her to instead of pushing her away. I tried to pull back a little bit but Donna scooted in closer to me. Then her hand went under my shirt. It felt so good to allow her to touch me that way. I'd never been with a woman before but I was a bit curious about her strap-on and how it would feel if she used it on me. I quickly came to my senses though and stopped kissing her.

"Donna, I'm very vulnerable right now. The only reason any of this is happening is because of how frustrated I am with Hunter. I really didn't mean to drag you into my drama."

"No apologies babe. I just hope you don't give all of yourself to him. Your acting career is really heading in a good direction. You really need to focus on your happiness, is all I'm saying."

Donna took another puff of her blunt and told me that my pants were in the living room. I had no clue how they'd gotten in there but I didn't want to talk anymore. I just wanted to get the hell out of there because the things I was beginning to envision Donna doing to me were freaking me out so I had to go.

"I'll call you when I get home."

I was so used to checking in with Hunter I guess it was just a habit to say that.

"Alright babe. Five o'clock rehearsal this evening."

108

"This evening? I thought we weren't back at it until tomorrow?"

"Nope."

"Dammit, by the time I drive all the way back home, it'll be time for me to come right back this way!"

"All the more reason you should just stay." Donna smiled.

"Like I said, I need to get home. I'll be back in time for rehearsal."

"Don't forget, your car is still parked by the club. Let me get my keys and I'll drive you over there."

I really didn't want to have to go all the way back home and come back this way but if I didn't, I probably would've ended up doing things with Donna I'd regret. All of this stressing I was doing over Hunter was starting to really take its toll on me. And the sad part was, he probably didn't even care.

* * *

Today was extremely frustrating. I'd driven all the way to Barrington just to find out that the buyer was no longer interested in the property and flaked out. Absolutely no call, no show. This is what infuriated me about buyers and why I preferred to work with sellers. My goal was to get as many listings as possible because in order to really make sustainable income in this business, you have to have a healthy list of homes that other real estate agents can sell for you. Which is what I needed in order to focus on my acting career.

When I got back home, Hunter still wasn't there after being out of town for the past week. Initially, he said he was heading out to Miami for a few days to visit one of his properties but clearly that trip lasted much longer than I anticipated. He was supposed to come home a few days ago but he texted me to let me know he still had some work to do and that he wouldn't make it back until the middle of the week. We hadn't really talked much either while he was gone because he always sounded rushed on the phone. I was so hungry from my long work day. If Hunter was home, I would've cooked but seeing that I was by myself, I decided to order in.

The house was quiet and it felt extremely empty without Hunter there. I put a pot on the stove to warm some water. As soon as the teapot whistled, I turned the burner off and put a teabag in my favorite mug, poured the hot water in and allowed it to steep. I told Alexa to play some jazz music and I walked into the sunroom. My Shih Tzu followed me and started sniffing my leg. Not only did she need some attention and affection, she could always tell when I needed it too.

I missed Hunter's presence and I wanted us to have real conversations about our marriage and how alone I'd been feeling lately. I wanted him to understand how much I needed his support when it came to my acting career. It's as if he was jealous of my success even though he was extremely successful in his own right. I also wanted us to work on our communication a bit more as I needed him to stop entertaining women in a way that made me feel uncomfortable. I get that he's always been surrounded by a plethora of women due to his work, but I wanted him to make me a priority and make me feel like all of those other women came secondary to me. I just wasn't getting that from him. I was always vying for his attention and it felt really unfair.

Again, he never actually admitted to cheating, but I knew he'd been with someone else and for some reason, it just felt like he was seeing someone in particular, especially with so many business trips popping up all of a sudden. I couldn't put my finger on it, but my intuition was definitely sending smoke signals these days. I had been growing more and more suspicious particularly because there was this Instagram model who started following me as she was also following Hunter. She started liking many of my photos, specifically the ones with Hunter and I. I rarely took social media too seriously because of what we did for a living. It was pretty common for us to have admirers, but this model was different.

Under one of our recent photos together, she commented, *"You're such a beautiful couple and I'm pretty sure you have great surprises in store."* Her comment seemed a bit cryptic but I didn't give it much attention. I started to let it go but when I went to her profile, the very last post she made was a reel of herself at a party. I could've sworn I saw Hunter in the background but the video went so fast that I couldn't tell. I tried playing it back several times but still no luck deciphering if it was him.

My computer was sitting on the table and even though I didn't want to think of doing anymore work for the rest of the day, I decided to follow up on a few listings. I checked my personal email first and what I discovered ripped me to pieces. In the subject line it read, *I thought you should know.* It was from an account from someone called Diabolical Babe. At first I thought it was spam but it didn't go to my junk folder which was strange to me. When I opened the email, there was a video attachment and as soon as I opened it, I saw Hunter lying in the bed in what clearly looked like a hotel suite. I heard someone singing in the background but I couldn't see who it was but it sounded like someone was in the suite with him. I started getting angry but I was also scared that something happened to him because I hadn't really talked to him the entire time he was out of town.

Finally, he started to move as if he was just waking up from a hangover. When he got out of the bed, he was completely naked. His ass and dick were exposed and a tear fell from my eyes because here was actual proof of my husband cheating. There were many times I sensed he was being unfaithful due to his stories and whereabouts not adding up, but he never flat out admitted to me that he was. It was apparent he'd been with a woman and whomever she was wanted me to know so she set up a camera in their hotel room to prove it.

Hunter slowly walked over to the drawers where there was a mirror above it. It looked like there was something on the mirror written in lipstick but I couldn't quite tell what it was. I heard him trying to read it through his grogginess but I couldn't hear him. A few seconds later, Hunter began screaming, "FUUUUUUCCCCKKKK" really loudly. He ran into the bathroom and walked back into the bedroom forcefully holding a woman's wrist while facing the mirror and screaming at her asking, "What the fuck is this shit?" I was trying so hard to zoom into the message on the mirror but I still couldn't tell what it read.

The woman started laughing uncontrollably and then Hunter grabbed her by the neck. I screamed because he started choking her and I was afraid he was going to kill her. She grabbed a vase from off the dresser from behind her and hit him on the head with it and he fell to the floor.

It was such a loud thump. I gasped and it felt like my heart stopped. She yelled at him saying, "Yes, I have AIDS and you have it too motherfucker!" And then she walked towards the camera as if she was looking at me dead in my eyes while pointing to the mirror and said, "You see that? It says, "Welcome to the world of AIDS, bitch." I couldn't believe it. I knew the tattoo on her arm looked really familiar. I didn't recognize her at first without the pounds of makeup on but then I realized it was the Instagram model. And then the screen went black.

I slammed my computer shut and I felt like I was having a panic attack as I started sweating and breathing at a rapid pace. It felt like it took hours for me to collect myself even though it was just a few minutes. If what this woman emailed me was really true, that would mean that I was infected too. No this can't be. I had my entire life ahead of me. I'd only been with seven men my entire life. I never had an STD, hell, I never even had stitches and now AIDS? All because of Hunter and him not being able to keep his dick in his pants? I screamed loudly and sobbed endlessly. I scared my Shih Tzu as she started whimpering as well. I wasn't even forty years old yet. How could this be happening to me? Was this a sick joke? This couldn't be real, but deep down, I felt it in the pit of my stomach that it was. I hated Hunter for doing this to me and I wanted to kill him. I continued to cry so much that I cried myself to sleep right at the table in the sunroom.

Hours later I was awakened by Hunter arriving back from his trip. He walked in the kitchen and touched my shoulder which startled me.

"Rose Marie, we need to talk." Hunter's face said it all.

"So now you want to talk?" I said rhetorically.

"So there's no other way to say this but——"

"You have AIDS, I know." I stared out the window and didn't even look at his face. "I was going to ask you how did you know but clearly that bitch got to you before I did." "I can't fucking believe you." I said in a low, yet stern tone of voice.

"Listen, the shit seemed unreal but I went to my buddy's office out in Miami who's a doctor and got tested. Fuck, I can't believe this shit!" Hunter slammed the table with his hand.

"All of the times I asked you if you were cheating on me and it has come to this?" I began to cry again and my hands were shaking.

"You just need to get tested." Hunter said matter of factly as if my feelings didn't even matter.

"So you're not going to even address the fact that you've been cheating on me for months, probably years and you've exposed me to an incurable disease? And all you have to say is you need to get tested? Are you serious? You have practically destroyed my life over some Instagram bitch? How could you?" I yelled.

I knew I was upset because I never raised my voice at Hunter after all of the years we'd been together.

"I'm not dealing with your shit right now. I have fucking AIDS and you probably have it too. That's the reality. Now get over your shit and just go get tested."

Hunter walked away and went upstairs to do God only knows what and I was left feeling alone again but this time, I wanted revenge.

* * *

I decided to take some time off work for a couple of weeks and I also told my agent I needed some time to sort some things out in my personal life. I was unable to concentrate on auditioning for anything right now. I didn't even tell Donna what was going on because I didn't want anyone to know. I felt scared, angry, frustrated, confused, and lonely. All I could think about was what I could have possibly done in my life to deserve this.

When I got the official call from my doctor with the test results, I felt like I'd been in a movie. To hear her say that I indeed had AIDS felt like a gut punch. I couldn't believe it as I didn't feel or look sick. I felt exactly the same as I always did so I questioned the results because I was still in a state of shock and denial. She asked me to come back to the office so that she could go over next steps with me after receiving my diagnosis.

Honestly, everything just felt like a blur. I wasn't even paying attention to what she was saying and her words just sounded muffled at one point. I just remember breaking down and crying in the exam room and her rubbing my back trying to console me. She had been my doctor for the past decade so she was well aware of my health history and I could tell she felt really sorry for me.

My tears then turned to anger all over again and every curse word I could muster up came out of my mouth.

"How the fuck could he do this to me?" I screamed.

My doctor continued to allow me to express myself in the way I needed to. I'm pretty sure she'd dealt with many people receiving various diagnoses that brought about a wide range of emotions and I was no different. My doctor told me that I could take as much time as I needed and she stepped out of the room to give me some time to myself.

I got up off the examination table and paced back and forth. I hadn't had sex with anyone else since being married to Hunter so I didn't have to disclose this information to any previous sex partners. I really wanted to call my mom and talk to her but I was so hurt and embarrassed. I literally went through the five stages of grief about three times in that office. I was a wreck and I just felt like how could I ever recover from this?

I wondered if Hunter even had the decency to tell the women he'd been sleeping with that he had AIDS. His assistant came to my mind because I just had a gut feeling he was sleeping with her. He'd spent so much time with her and always passed it off as business but I could tell the dynamic between them. And the sad part is that I think she actually really liked him. She couldn't have been no more than twenty-five years old. It was a damn shame that I was actually concerned about her while I was dealing with this myself. I hated feeling this way but I really wanted Hunter to suffer in the worst way and I wanted to be the one to make it happen.

I wiped my tears and decided once I left the doctor's office that day, I would be sure to pay Hunter back for this. I didn't know how but I was determined by any means necessary.

* * *

I ended up telling Donna about my diagnosis and she was livid. Even though I knew it wouldn't change my situation, I was glad that someone was on my side who was just as outraged as I was. I worried that she would look at me funny or treat me differently when I initially told her but nothing had changed at all. She really looked out for me and kept me abreast of what was going on during rehearsals. She warded off any questions and redirected conversations amongst cast members so they wouldn't start gossiping about me and making me feel like an outcast. It was so strange to be in this position. Things like this just didn't happen to me and now I could become the poster child for someone with AIDS. Life seemed so unfair.

I disclosed to Donna that I was so angry that I could choke Hunter with my bare hands and I wanted to get my revenge. She said she knew I was upset for me to say something like that because it was so out of my character. I told her that I wasn't bluffing and that I was serious about watching him die. That's how angry I was that he exposed me to a deadly disease.

One day Donna asked me to meet up with her at a secret location but she didn't say what it was about. We ended up meeting in a private room in a club and she mentioned that she had a good friend who worked in pharmaceuticals. She gave me a bottle that contained only two pills. When I asked her what it was, she told me to just make sure I dropped the tablets in Hunter's drink and within a matter or an hour or so of consuming it, he would doze off and succumb to a fatal heart attack. We stared at each other in silence and I wondered if I could be that cold but he had already ruined my life so what did I have to lose?

The countdown to his demise seemed like forever until that day had officially arrived. I prepared breakfast while Hunter took a shower. We really hadn't talked at all since he came home from his trip two weeks ago and nonchalantly delivered the news to me that he had AIDS. I was so detached from myself and I didn't have any remorse for what I was about to do. I felt completely justified in not only wanting to wipe him off the face of the earth, but wanting to watch him die right before my eyes.

I heard Hunter walking down the stairs and I turned into the actress that I was and whispered, "show time" to myself.

"I made some scrambled eggs, toast, and sausages if you want any?" I asked dryly because if I would've expressed any other emotion, it would've seemed suspicious to him.

"I was thinking of just grabbing some breakfast on my way to the office so, no thanks."

Hunter grabbed his suit jacket off of the kitchen counter.

All I could think to myself was this bastard just continues to go on with his life like he didn't have a care in the world but I had to think fast because I needed him to ingest these pills today.

"Look, we don't have to talk for you to eat breakfast. As a matter of fact, I don't have anything to say to you either but you might as well eat something." I tried to sound convincing.

"Okay fine. I have to hurry up and meet Vanessa because she has escrow documents for me that I was expecting to be signed." Hunter said while sitting at the kitchen table scarfing down his breakfast.

"So speaking of Vanessa, your assistant, have you told her that you have AIDS?" I asked casually.

"What the fuck is wrong with you? Why would you ask me that?" Hunter said with an elevated tone.

"Well, I'm pretty sure you were cheating on me with her. She's so young and now you've messed up her life too." I was getting angry all over again and I wanted to stick it to Hunter any way that I could.

"Vanessa's a big girl and if she wants to play in the big leagues, she needs to be prepared for however that turns out." Hunter continued to eat his breakfast like he could care less how evil he was.

"I can't believe how cold and uncaring you are. You don't think about anyone but yourself!" I screamed.

"I'm not getting into this with you this morning." Hunter continued to eat his food and I could tell he was looking by the sink for something to drink.

This was my chance. Hunter continued to give me more ammunition to poison his ass and watch him collapse. He hurt me so badly and he was going to feel my pain one way or another. I turned around and faced the window and discreetly dropped the two pills in his orange juice and then the doorbell rang. Shit, who could be coming to our house at seven-thirty in the morning? Hunter started to get up to answer the door but I needed him to take the pills first. I placed the glass of orange juice on the table next to Hunter's plate.

"Who could that be?" I questioned.

Hunter just ignored me and walked to the door. I heard a woman's voice that sounded like Vanessa. I thought he was meeting her so why was she here at our house? It's not like she hadn't dropped off papers before but never this early.

"Hi Rose Marie." Vanessa said with a blank look on her face that I couldn't quite figure out.

"Oh hi, Vanessa. I didn't expect to see you here, especially this early in the morning." I sort of rolled my eyes.

"Are you all done with all this female bonding? Vanessa, I said I was going to meet you at the office but seeing that you're here, where are those escrow documents I asked for?"

Vanessa didn't seem bothered at all by Hunter's attitude and just handed him the documents like it was nothing. Maybe she had become accustomed to the way he talked down to people and just accepted it. I mean she was only twenty-five years old. Maybe she didn't really think she deserved to be treated any better.

"Rose Marie, if it's okay, can I have some orange juice? I'm sorry to interrupt your breakfast. I'm just a bit thirsty."

"Uum, sure?"

I poured her a glass of orange juice and gave it to her. My heart began racing a bit because I knew this was the only time to make this happen. I spaced out for a minute and my mind began to wander to the time I met Hunter. I thought if I had never given him my number maybe I wouldn't be in this situation now.

"I'm heading out for a run. You two enjoy your day." I said sarcastically.

As I approached the front door, Vanessa ended up following me and meeting me outside.

"Uum, can I help you Vanessa?" I said with an attitude.

What could she possibly want to talk to me about? I wanted nothing to do with her. She needed to leave so that Hunter would drink the juice and I could watch him die like I planned.

"I just wanted to say Hunter is a piece of shit! You've probably known this but Hunter and I have been fucking for the past year. He told me he loved me and that he was going to leave you to be with me and I actually believed him. He didn't even have the decency to tell me he had AIDS. I found out from a routine blood test I had done and he was the only person I'd been with for the past year. He doesn't even know that I know. He's worthless and deserves to die."

"First of all, how dare you come to my house and accuse my husband of cheating, and having AIDS too? Are you out of your mind? I'm going for my run and when I get back, you better be gone from my house." I tried to sound convincing as I didn't want Vanessa to know that I knew about the diagnosis as well as me plotting to kill Hunter. I needed no one to think I was responsible or even capable of such a thing.

"Like I said, he deserves to die and if you want to be oblivious to who he is, that's on you."

Vanessa walked back inside my house and had the nerve to slam my door. I took off running as I was furious! I felt another side of me starting to rise and I wanted to scream. Not only had the Instagram model confronted me through video, but now Vanessa? I could only imagine who else would come out of the woodworks regarding Hunter's illicit affairs. The more I ran, the angrier I got. Maybe it was a good thing she was still at the house with Hunter so that when he drank his juice, she would be there with him and then the cops would think she was responsible. This plan was working out better than I expected until it hit me that I'd poured two glasses of orange juice. There was no way they would be able to tell them both apart!

I stopped dead in my tracks as I was out of breath not only from running but from the thought that Vanessa might actually drink from the wrong cup. I turned back around and started running towards my house. Oh my God, please let me get back in time and fix this. The poison was intended for Hunter, not Vanessa. I continued to speed up and by the time I got back to my front door, it was cracked open. Vanessa's car was still outside. So many thoughts raced through my head as I tiptoed back into the house as I didn't hear any sounds or voices. Where was Vanessa?

I slowly walked into the kitchen and noticed Hunter's feet first, kind of curved to the side. I could feel myself growing more nervous as I still didn't hear any sounds. As I got closer, I noticed Hunter looked a bit slumped over and sure enough his face was lying in his plate and the escrow documents were on the floor. I touched Hunter's neck to see if I could feel a pulse and there was absolutely nothing. Clearly my plan worked, but where was Vanessa?

"Vanessa! Where are you? Are you still here?" I yelled.

Then I screamed when I looked at the table at what appeared to be two full glasses of orange juice still there. Wait a minute? Did he drink it? Did Vanessa drink it?

I ran through every part of my home looking for Vanessa and couldn't find her. I even went back outside to check her car and she wasn't in there. What the hell? I was so scared and couldn't figure out who killed Hunter? It didn't look like he drank the juice that I poured him and Vanessa was nowhere to be found.

I knew I would never be the same after this. I still had to live with this disease but also live with the fact that I'd never know who killed Hunter. One thing is for sure, life can truly be a twisted game and I was dealt a crazy hand but I wasn't going to stop until Hunter felt the wrath one way or another. Clearly he met his demise.

Printed in the USA
CPSIA information can be obtained
at www.ICGtesting.com
JSHW020041140923
48385JS00006B/13

9 781088 295649